P9-AFV-743

THE SHERIFF TAKES A W

THE SHERIFF TAKES A WIFE

WITHDRAWN

DEBBIE MACOMBER

CONTRA COSTA COUNTY LIBRARY

THORNDIKE
CHIVERS

3 1901 04423 5499

This Large Print edition is published by Thorndike Press, Waterville, Maine, USA and by BBC Audiobooks Ltd, Bath, England.
Thorndike Press, a part of Gale, Cengage Learning.
Copyright © 1990 by Debbie Macomber.
The moral right of the author has been asserted.

ALL RIGHTS RESERVED
This is a work of fiction. Names, characters, places, and incidents are either the product of the author's imagination or are used fictitiously, and any resemblance to actual persons, living or dead, business establishments, events, or locales is entirely coincidental.
The text of this Large Print edition is unabridged.
Other aspects of the book may vary from the original edition.
Set in 16 pt. Plantin.
Printed on permanent paper.

LIBRARY OF CONGRESS CATALOGING-IN-PUBLICATION DATA

Macomber, Debbie.
   The sheriff takes a wife : the Manning sisters / by Debbie Macomber.
      p. cm. — (Thorndike Press large print romance)
   ISBN-13: 978-1-4104-0836-5 (hardcover : alk. paper)
   ISBN-10: 1-4104-0836-1 (hardcover : alk. paper)
   1. Sheriffs—Fiction. 2. Women teachers—Fiction. 3. Ranchers—Fiction. 4. Montana—Fiction. 5. Large type books. I. Title.
   PS3563.A2364S445 2008
   813'.54—dc22
                                               2008027424

BRITISH LIBRARY CATALOGUING-IN-PUBLICATION DATA AVAILABLE

Published in 2008 in the U.S. by arrangement with Harlequin Books S.A.
Published in 2009 in the U.K. by arrangement with Harlequin Enterprises II B.V.

U.K. Hardcover: 978 1 408 42137 6 (Chivers Large Print)
U.K. Softcover: 978 1 408 42138 3 (Camden Large Print)

Printed in the United States of America
1 2 3 4 5 6 7 12 11 10 09 08

DEAR FRIENDS,

Early in my writing career I met a special reader named Ginny Manning. She was a feisty woman, raised in (believe it or not) a jailhouse in eastern Washington, not far from my hometown of Yakima. She liked my books and encouraged me as a writer. I occasionally met with her over the next few years, and when I decided to write a series of books revolving around a large family, I called that family Manning, after my friend Ginny. The Manning Family series, five books in all (together with a sixth connected story), delighted my friend, who took great pride in the fact that I'd chosen her name.

Ginny came to visit me last summer and was as spirited as I remembered. She was a bit slower — she was in her eighties, after all — but it was the same wonderful Ginny. Just a couple of weeks later, one of her sons wrote to tell me his mother had been diagnosed with cancer. Ginny died shortly thereafter. I realize now that she came to tell me goodbye.

It gives me real pleasure to see the Manning Family books reissued after nearly twenty years. The first two, *The Cowboy's Lady* and *The Sheriff Takes a Wife,* feature the Manning girls. The books have been refreshed and updated, but Russ Palmer and his friend Sheriff Cody Franklin are still as opinionated ·(and yes, chauvinistic) as ever, and it takes two Manning women to show these cowboys the light. I know my friend Ginny would be pleased to see a whole new generation of readers discovering "her" stories.

I invite you to enter the world of Montana men and Manning women!

Debbie Macomber

P.S. I love to hear from my readers. You can reach me at www.debbiemacomber.com or P.O. Box 1458, Port Orchard, WA 98366.

To Merrily Boone
Friend
Title Finder
Speller of Impossible Words
Discoverer of Great Restaurants

ONE

"What do you *mean* you're in labor?" Christy Manning asked her sister.

"I didn't say that . . . exactly," Taylor Palmer said, her palms flattened against her protruding abdomen. She lowered her eyelashes, taking a long, slow breath.

"You can't be in labor! I just got here. My suitcases are still in the trunk of my car." Christy bolted to her feet and shoved the dark curls away from her face with both hands. She'd been driving for nearly three days to be with her sister for the birth of this baby, but she hadn't counted on the blessed event happening quite so soon.

"What do you want me to do?" she asked, regaining her poise. In her opinion, there was plenty of reason for alarm. The Lazy P, Russ and Taylor's cattle ranch, was miles outside Cougar Point, the closest town. And there wasn't a neighbor in sight.

Taylor's husband, Russ, was driving his

sister, Mandy, over to a friend's house and doing a couple of errands before heading back to the ranch. At most he'd be gone only an hour, or so he'd claimed.

But a lot could happen in an hour.

"I'm not convinced this is the real thing," Taylor said in an apparent effort to reassure Christy, but her hands caressed her stomach as she spoke. "I've never been in labor before, so I'm not exactly sure what to expect."

Trying to gather her scattering wits, Christy circled the kitchen table. First and foremost, she needed to keep calm. Mentally she reviewed the recent classes she'd taken through the local library. She knew CPR and enough karate to defend herself. Great. She could knock someone out and then revive him. A lot of good either of those skills was going to do her in this situation.

She swallowed a feeling of impending panic. She wasn't even supposed to be in Montana. Her mother was the one who'd planned to make the trip, only Elizabeth Manning had taken a fall and broken her leg. She was having trouble getting around and would be little or no help to Taylor. Since Christy had a couple of weeks of vacation due, she'd volunteered to come and stay with her sister. It wasn't any sacrifice on her part; Christy and Taylor had always been close.

Unfortunately no one had bothered to tell her she was going to be stuck alone on a cattle ranch with her nine months' pregnant sister, who was "feeling funny."

It all seemed unreal. Christy had arrived late the night before. Too late to do more than greet everyone, haul her overnight bag into the guest bedroom and fall exhausted into bed.

"Stop looking like you expect to deliver this baby on your own," Taylor said, smiling up at her sister.

"But, Miss Scarlett, I don't know nothin' about birthin' no babies," Christy wailed in a Southern drawl. She might be teasing, but what she said was the honest-to-goodness truth.

None of this was supposed to be happening — at least not like this. Taylor should be living in Seattle with the rest of her family. Instead, Christy's older sister had gone to Montana a year earlier and to everyone's surprise married a cattle rancher three months later.

At the time, Christy couldn't imagine what had possessed her cultured, cosmopolitan sister to marry someone like Russ Palmer. Especially in Reno, without a single

11

family member present.

Their father hadn't been pleased at being cheated out of the chance to walk his daughter down the aisle, but once he'd met Russ, the rancher had won him over. Russ had reassured everyone in the family without even trying. Taylor and her husband had flown to Seattle at the end of May to celebrate her parents' wedding anniversary. It was then that he'd met Christy and her three brothers.

Taylor winced and her eyes drifted shut again. Her display of pain effectively cut off Christy's thoughts. She held her breath until she saw the tension slowly ease from her sister's body. "What happened?"

"I felt a funny pain, that's all. Don't worry. It wasn't anything."

"A funny pain? And you don't want me to worry?" Christy echoed. She couldn't keep the panic out of her voice. "Then why do I have this urge to boil water?"

Taylor, forever calm and serene in a crisis, grinned. "Don't worry. I've been having these pains off and on for the past week, but . . ."

"But what?" Christy asked.

"But these feel . . . different. I don't know how to explain it." She rose haltingly to her feet. "I think it might be a good idea if I got dressed."

"Right," Christy said, as if the idea was a stroke of genius. "Me, too." With her arm around what remained of Taylor's waist, Christy led her sister down the hallway that went to the master bedroom. "Do you need any help?"

"Don't be ridiculous!" Almost before the words had left her lips, Taylor let out a cry and pressed one shoulder to the wall while clutching her stomach.

Christy was instantly alarmed. "What is it?"

"Oh . . . my." Wide-eyed, Taylor turned toward Christy. "Hurry and get some towels. My water just broke."

"Your water broke," Christy repeated in a stupor. She threw her hands toward the ceiling. "Her water just broke." Rushing into the bathroom, she returned with enough towels to soak up a flood.

Taylor was still leaning against the wall, breathing deeply, her eyes closed. Christy dropped the towels onto the floor, far more concerned about Taylor than she was about a little water. "Are you all right?"

Her sister answered with a nod that said otherwise.

"I'm calling the doctor," Christy told her. "Don't you dare move. Understand?" The

13

panic was stronger than ever, but Christy managed to swallow it. Taylor needed her; there wasn't time to be concerned with her own fears.

Taylor's doctor was in Miles City, sixty miles away, and the hospital was there, too. As far as she could tell, they were an hour or more from help. Christy spoke to Dr. Donovan briefly, and when she explained what had happened, the doctor suggested Taylor come to the hospital immediately.

"I'm not going without Russ," Taylor insisted when Christy relayed her conversation. "Russ will be back any minute."

Christy started to balk. It wasn't her fault that Taylor's husband had such a bad sense of timing.

"You don't know Russ the way I do," Taylor said, even before Christy had a chance to reason with her. "If he came home and found us gone —"

"I'll leave him a note. He'll understand. Then as soon as he's back, he can join us."

"No."

Christy had heard that tone of voice often enough to realize these was no way she could budge that stubborn streak of Taylor's. "We can't just sit here and wait," Christy moaned.

"Of course we can. Now relax!"

"Me, relax? You're the one having the baby."

"I'm fine. Baby Palmer and mother are both calm and prepared."

Baby Palmer. Her only sister was about to become a mother. This wasn't new information, but until this moment Taylor's pregnancy had seemed abstract. Yet here they were alone together, and suddenly this baby was very real. This tiny life depended on Christy, and the thought was terrifying. Yet nothing she said would convince Taylor to leave for the hospital without Russ.

The next thirty minutes felt like thirty years. Christy changed into jeans and a sweatshirt, forced down another cup of coffee and looked out the kitchen window every three seconds.

Outwardly Taylor still seemed calm, but Christy could tell from the pain that flashed on her sister's face that the intensity of the contractions was increasing.

"Maybe you should call the feed store. If Russ isn't there, then contact Cody."

"Great idea!" Christy leaped at the possibility of bringing someone else into the picture. The sooner the better. "Just a minute," she said. "Who's Cody?"

"Cody Franklin . . . he's the newly elected sheriff and a good friend. I don't know what his schedule is, so try the office first. If he's not at work, his home number's written in the front of the phone book."

Calling anyone, including the National Guard, sounded like an excellent plan to Christy. She found the impossibly thin phone book in the drawer. Good grief, she'd ordered from menus thicker than this.

Christy phoned the feed store first. The lady who answered said Russ had left a half hour earlier, and she hadn't a clue where he'd gone. Christy accepted this with a shrug. At the rate things were developing, she was about to take an advanced course in childbirth.

Christy found the sheriff's home number right where Taylor said it would be. She punched it out and waited impatiently for someone, anyone, to answer.

"Hello," a groggy voice muttered on the fourth ring.

"Hi, oh, thank God you answered." Christy was so relieved, she wanted to weep. She gulped in one giant breath and rushed to explain. "You don't know me. I'm Christy Manning, Taylor Palmer's sister, and Russ left an hour ago and promised he'd be back but he isn't and Taylor's water broke and she's in labor. She keeps insisting she won't leave for the hospital until Russ comes

16

home, but he isn't here, and I don't know anything about delivering babies."

A short silence followed. "Taylor's in labor?"

"That's what I just finished saying. The second and equally important factor is that Russ, the father of this about-to-be-born-baby, isn't here. He said he'd only be gone an hour, but he's late, and Taylor really should be leaving for the hospital."

"Where did he say he was going?"

"The feed store. But he left there thirty minutes ago and . . . and *disappeared.*" That might be an exaggeration, but the situation called for a minor stretching of the truth, although she realized she'd made it sound as if he'd been abducted by aliens.

"I'll find him and be there as soon as I can."

The relief that washed over Christy felt like a cool evening rain after the hottest day of summer. Taylor needed her, and the last thing Christy wanted to do was reveal how much this situation frightened her. She'd made this trip to help Taylor with the baby. As in diaper, hold, burp. Not *deliver.*

She coaxed Taylor into the living room and had her lie down on the sofa. The ease with which Christy was able to convince her revealed a great deal about Taylor's condition. Although she struggled to disguise it, her dauntless older sister was scared. The pains were obviously far stronger than Taylor was willing to admit.

A whole lifetime seemed to pass before Christy heard a car barreling down the driveway. Taylor sighed audibly and relaxed against the pillows Christy had placed behind her back. "That's Russ now."

Christy hurried to the back door. She didn't recognize the car as Russ's, but that was the least of her worries. The four-wheel-drive Cherokee hadn't even come to a stop before her brother-in-law leaped out of the front seat.

He raced up the steps. "Where's Taylor?" he demanded.

Numb with relief, Christy sagged against the doorjamb and pointed toward the living room. She was about to follow her brother-in-law when a second man climbed out of the driver's seat.

Christy couldn't pull her eyes away from this tall, long-limbed stranger. It was all she could do not to throw her arms around him in thanks. "You must be Cody."

He touched the rim of his Stetson. "At your service. You must be Taylor's sister," he said, sauntering toward her.

"Christy Manning," she said in an authoritative voice, as if she had the situation completely under control and frequently delivered babies while vacationing. She stepped forward to offer the sheriff of Custer County her hand. In truth she was so grateful he'd found Russ that she was close to tears.

A few seconds later, Russ came out, carrying Taylor. "You ready?" he asked his friend.

"Russ, put me down," Taylor insisted. "I'm too heavy."

"We'll argue later, but at the moment you're about to give birth to my son," Russ reminded her with a worried frown.

"Our baby could very well be a girl," Taylor began. "You're still so pigheaded you refuse to —"

"I swear you're the only woman on God's green earth who'd argue with me at a time like this."

"I'd think you'd be used to it by now," Taylor mumbled, but her voice faded as a fresh contraction overtook her. She closed her eyes, pressed her hands to her belly and breathed deeply.

Russ's distraught gaze connected with Christy's.

"I'll get her suitcase," Christy said as she rushed into the master bedroom. When she reappeared, Cody took the single bag from her hands and put it inside the car. Taylor and Russ were already situated in the back seat, and the passenger door was open for Christy. Without another word, she climbed inside and snapped the seat belt in place.

The ride to the hospital took a full hour. Christy didn't need to look at the speedometer to know Cody was traveling well above the speed limit. If anything, she had to stop herself from pleading with him to go even faster.

Taylor did an admirable job of disguising the extent of her discomfort, but it was apparent to all that the sooner she was under medical supervision the better. Russ was calm and collected.

It turned out that the carburetor in Russ's truck had started acting up, and he'd pulled over to the side of the road. Cody had found him bent over the engine, trying to fix it so he could make it back to the ranch.

Christy held herself tense until they reached the outskirts of Miles City. Only then did she feel herself start to relax.

Within ten minutes of their arrival at the hospital, Taylor was in the labor room with Russ at her side. Cody and Christy were relegated to the waiting room, where they leafed through six-month-old issues of *Time* magazine.

Soon bored with those, Christy found her gaze wandering to Cody. Fine lines fanned out from the corners of his dark eyes, and sharply cut grooves bracketed his mouth. He was tanned, his skin weathered by the sun and wind. He had the kind of rich bronze coloring that others strived to achieve under a sunlamp. His hair was thick and as dark as his eyes and cut military short. He wasn't handsome or stunning or anything else she could easily put a name to, but he was beyond a doubt the most uncompromisingly masculine man she'd ever seen. Immediately she experienced a faint stirring of guilt.

James. Dear, sweet James. Always so patient and understanding. She shouldn't even be *looking* at another man, not when she had James.

Cody glanced up from his magazine, and their eyes met. Christy managed to fake a smile. He returned it with a smile of his own and went back to reading. Christy made a pretense of doing the same thing. Despite her best efforts, her gaze wandered back to the sheriff again and again. It was somewhat embarrassing to realize that she wasn't studying him as a representative of law and order but as a man. Cody Franklin was incredibly male. Incredibly . . . incredible. Everything about him spoke of strength and purpose: his walk, the square set of his jaw, even the way he sat with his ankle resting over his knee. Disturbed by her unintended focus on the sheriff, she flipped through the pages of a two-year-old issue of *People.* Something was definitely wrong with her. No doubt it had to do with Taylor and the baby. Babies were said to stir up lots of feelings and buried emotions. What astonished her was that she should find this man so attractive.

Enough!

More determined than ever, Christy reached for another magazine and gazed unseeing at its pages.

"I take it you just arrived in Cougar Point?" Cody surprised her by asking.

"Last night," Christy said, setting aside the dog-eared issue of *People.* "Actually, it was early this morning when I went to bed. Russ left the house about the time I came down for coffee, and the next thing I knew, Taylor was telling me she was having these 'funny' pains, only I wasn't laughing, and neither was she."

"How long after that did you call me?"

"Too long," Christy said vehemently. "Taylor claimed the pains were nothing to worry about. I knew I shouldn't have listened to her. Good grief, what does she know?"

Cody smiled, and her eyes were immediately drawn to his full sensual mouth. Frustrated with herself, she quickly looked away.

"Don't be so hard on yourself. You handled the situation exactly the way you should have." He turned back to the periodical. Christy picked up another one herself, but when she glanced up, she saw Cody studying her. "I don't mean to stare," he apologized, "but I can't get over how much you and Taylor resemble each other."

That was almost worth a laugh. She'd hardly been able to keep her eyes off Cody Franklin from the moment they got to the hospital, and *he* was apologizing for staring at *her!* As for the part about the two sisters looking alike, Christy took that as a compliment. Taylor was stunning. In fact, Christy couldn't remember a time when her sister had been more beautiful than she was right now. Taylor was the beauty, not Christy. She didn't mean to sell herself short; she knew she was reasonably attractive. Perhaps the biggest difference was that Taylor had spunk. Her older sister had always displayed such tenacity, such mettle. When it came to dealing with their headstrong father, Taylor had more courage than the rest of them put together.

Anyone looking at the two sisters would know they were related; Christy was willing to grant the sheriff that much. Their deep blue eyes were a distinct family trait, also shared by their three older brothers, as was the slightly upturned nose.

The two sisters styled their hair differently. Taylor kept her thick chestnut hair long, whereas Christy preferred hers short in a breezy wash-and-wear style.

Christy was about to make some comment along the lines of what a peaceful community Cougar Point seemed to be when they saw Russ.

Cody and Christy stood as Russ approached, his eyes slightly dazed.

"Taylor's ready to go into the delivery room."

"So soon?" Christy's heart was in her throat. "We just got here." She paused long enough to check her watch — and restrain her panic. "We've only been here twenty minutes. How could she possibly be ready for the delivery room?"

"I don't know. ... . The nurse told me the baby's coming *now*."

"It wasn't supposed to be this soon."

Russ wiped a hand down his face. "You're telling me? If Cody hadn't found me when he did . . ." He left the rest unsaid, but the implication was obvious.

Christy slumped back into the chair, her knees about to buckle. From everything she'd read and heard, babies were supposed to take their time, especially the first one. What about those twenty-hour labors her friends had described in minute detail? What about all the talk of first labors dragging on and on? Apparently Taylor hadn't been listening.

Russ returned to the double doors, then looked back into the waiting room. He swallowed hard, and Christy realized that if she'd been shaken by the news, it had affected Russ far more profoundly.

"Are you all right?" Cody asked her.

"Of course," she lied. "I'm not the one who's having a baby minutes after I arrive at the hospital." A fact for which Christy was eternally grateful. She wasn't nearly as courageous as Taylor; in fact, when it came right down to it, she considered herself a watered-down version of her older sister. All her life Christy had admired Taylor, wanting to be more like her. Instead, she was complacent and congenial, never causing her parents a moment's concern. Their father once claimed he owed every gray hair on his head to Taylor and every laugh line to Christy. His two daughters were the joy of his life, he often said.

"You look like you're going to faint," Cody said, watching her closely.

"Don't be ridiculous," she snapped, then instantly regretted her sharp tongue. She darted Cody an apologetic smile.

"Come on," Cody suggested, "let's walk. It'll help pass the time."

"Pass what time?" she muttered. "We've been here for about twenty minutes, and already Taylor's being wheeled into the delivery room."

"Come on, you could do with some activity — get your circulation going."

Christy merely nodded. Emotions were coming at her from every direction. Her first concern was for Taylor and the baby. The thought of this precious life, created in love, stirred a realm of deep feelings inside Christy. Her stomach started churning, her palms were sweating, and her heart seemed to be doing a jig. She couldn't have uttered a word had her life depended on it.

They walked the entire length of the hallway and stopped in front of the nursery. Christy carefully studied the row of newborns swaddled in pink and blue blankets and unexpectedly found tears clouding her eyes. Normally she wasn't sentimental or weepy. She didn't dare look over at Cody. He'd assume . . . She hadn't a clue what he'd assume, but it wouldn't be good.

"Christy?"

"The babies are really beautiful, aren't they?" she whispered, her gaze on the five infants.

"Yes, they are," he answered softly. He stood behind her and rested his hands on the curve of her shoulders. His touch was light, but it offered her a steadiness and comfort that had been lacking all morning. He didn't say anything when she brushed the telltale moisture from her cheeks, and Christy was grateful.

She didn't know what had come over her in the past few hours. She turned to face Cody, placed her hands on his forearms and stared up at him, her eyes bright with unshed tears.

Nothing seemed real anymore. It was as if she'd been walking around in a dream. A living fantasy was beginning to unfold right before her. Perhaps she'd spent too many hours on the road. Otherwise she wouldn't be looking into the darkest brown eyes she'd ever seen and thinking the things she was thinking.

Cody was staring back at her with the same wonder and surprise. He seemed about to say something important when the doors at the other end of the hall opened and Russ stepped out, wearing a green surgical gown and a large smile. Seeing him, both Christy and Cody rushed forward.

"It's a boy," Russ announced, his eyes shimmering with tears. He let out a wild shout of joy, grabbed a shocked Christy around the waist and boisterously whirled her around.

"Congratulations," Cody said, coming forward. The two men exchanged hearty handshakes, then hugged, slapping each other on the back.

Russ didn't speak for a moment and seemed to be composing himself. "He weighed in at eight pounds, three ounces, and he's the ugliest little critter you ever saw. Taylor kept saying how beautiful he is, and all I could see was this furious pink face bawling as loud as anything. His legs were pumping like an oil rig. That boy is madder than a wet wasp."

Christy felt tears in her eyes as she pressed her fingers to her lips. "How's Taylor?"

"She's fine . . . more than fine. That woman's incredible. I don't know what I ever did to deserve her, but I intend to thank God every day for the rest of my life." He half turned toward the doors he'd come through. "I've got to get back. They're taking Eric into the nursery now, and the delivery room nurse said I could watch him being washed and dressed. If I have anything to say about it, I'll do the washing and dressing myself."

"You're naming him Eric?" Christy asked as she moved one step forward.

Russ nodded. "Eric Russell, after your father and me. Taylor insists."

"That sounds like a perfectly wonderful name to me," Christy whispered, surprised at the emotion that clogged her throat. Her father would be so proud, the buttons would pop right off his shirt.

"If you two walk over to the nursery, you might be able to see him, too," Russ added excitedly. "Taylor will be out of the delivery room anytime. I know she'll want to talk to you both, so stick around for a little bit, okay?"

Christy and Cody had already started in that direction when Russ stopped them. "Hey, one last thing. Taylor and I talked it over, and we want the two of you to be Eric's godparents."

Christy exchanged a meaningful glance

29

with Cody before they simultaneously nodded.

"We'd be honored," Cody answered for
them.

"Truly honored," Christy repeated, her
throat tightening even more.

In her excitement Christy whirled around
to face Cody — except that she hadn't realized he was quite so close. She flattened
her hands against his chest as she smiled up
at him, her joy overflowing now that her
nephew was safely born.

Cody returned the smile. His dark eyes
were alive with emotion.

Slowly, moving as if he were hypnotized,
Cody slipped his arms around her waist and
raised her from the ground. Her hands
clutched his shirt collar as his eyes delved
into hers.

"I believe congratulations are in order,
don't you?"

"Yes," she said, hugging him, afraid he was
going to kiss her, equally afraid he wouldn't.

How would she ever explain kissing another man to James? How would she ratio-
nalize allowing Cody to hold her like this
when she'd promised to spend her life loving someone else?

Two

"Oh, Taylor, he's so beautiful," Christy whispered. "Russ held him up for me to see and . . ." She paused, unable to continue. The minute she'd seen Eric, her heart had swollen with such a profound sense of love that it had been impossible to suppress her tears.

"You're crying," Taylor said softly.

Christy rubbed her cheeks. She reached for her sister, and they hugged with an intensity she'd never felt before. This wealth of emotion, of happiness, took Christy by storm.

"I love you, Taylor. I really do. And I love Eric, too. He's beautiful, perfect. I feel absolutely ecstatic." She straightened and gave a breathy laugh. "I want to throw open the windows and tell the world my sister just had a beautiful baby boy."

"Did you get a chance to talk to Mom and Dad?"

Christy nodded. The moment her mother heard the news she'd started weeping and then her father had taken the phone. His own voice hadn't sounded all that steady, either. Russ had done most of the talking with Christy crowded close beside him. When it was her turn, she seemed to jabber on like a magpie, but couldn't stop herself.

Following the conversation, Russ and Cody had gone to the hospital gift shop to buy a box of cigars. Christy had spent these few moments alone with her sister.

"I'm sorry I frightened you," Taylor said apologetically, "but I didn't want to leave for the hospital without Russ."

"I understood. I wasn't worried." On the contrary, Christy had been nearly frantic, but it didn't matter now that everything had turned out so well.

Her sister sighed. "I'm glad you were able to meet Cody."

At the mention of the other man's name, Christy abruptly looked away, feeling uneasy. She hadn't had the chance to tell Taylor and Russ about her engagement to James Wilkens. Unfortunately the diamond ring James had given her was still at the jeweler's being sized. If she'd been wearing the ring, it would've been a logical introduction to her announcement. She'd meant to surprise her sister and brother-in-law with the big news as soon as she'd arrived, but it had been so late and everyone was exhausted. Then, before Christy knew it, it was morning and Taylor had gone into labor.

Now the timing was all wrong. Tomorrow, she promised herself, she'd tell Taylor. Everything would be less hectic then. But even as she formed that decision, Christy hesitated, not fully understanding why.

Her head spun and her thoughts skidded to a halt. Who did she think she was fooling?

She *did* know why.

Cody Franklin had hugged her when Russ had come to tell them about Eric. Now, an hour later, the way she'd felt in his arms still caused her pulse to accelerate. He'd pulled her close, and the feeling of being held by this man was completely and utterly natural, as instinctive as breathing or sleeping. It was as if they'd known each other all their lives. As if their relationship was one of long standing.

Without his saying a thing, Christy knew he'd experienced the same lavish range of sensations. They'd stared openly at each other, neither speaking. If Russ hadn't been there, Christy couldn't help wondering what would've happened. What they would've said to each other. If anything.

But Russ had been there, and after an awkward moment, Cody had released her. He'd dropped his arms with a reluctance that sent blood pounding through her veins until she grew dizzy simply remembering.

James was her fiancé! Yet she had to struggle to bring his image to mind. Her parents had been thrilled with the news of their engagement, but Christy had known they would be. Her father had told her often enough that James, an attorney, would make her an excellent husband. They'd been dating on and off for nearly two years, almost from the first week Christy had been hired as a paralegal at James's law firm. Their relationship, however, hadn't turned serious until three months ago. Until then, their dates had been casual get-togethers with mutual friends. Then they'd started working together on an important case. It had been a real coup for James to be assigned to defend Gary Mulligan against the Internal Revenue Service, and if everything went well, it could mean a partnership for him.

"Christy?"

She turned to her sister. "Sorry. Were you saying something?"

"Just that I'm glad you met Cody today."

"He . . . seems very nice," Christy answered, and sighed with relief when the nurse walked into the room, distracting her sister's attention from the subject of the sheriff. The woman brought in a huge bouquet of red roses in a tall crystal vase.

"Oh, my," Taylor breathed, reaching for the card. She tore open the small envelope and read the message. Immediate tears filled her eyes. "They're from Russ."

"How sweet."

Taylor smiled softly as a faraway look came into her eyes. Christy speculated that her sister was recalling the first time she'd met Russ and all that had happened since. Russ might not have been the man her family would've chosen for Taylor, but one fact had been clear from the instant they flew to Seattle to attend their parents' anniversary party. Russ Palmer loved Taylor. Beyond question. Beyond doubt. Whatever reservations Christy and her brothers held regarding this marriage had been quickly dissolved.

Footsteps from behind Christy told her Russ and Cody had returned.

"Russ . . ." Taylor held out her arms to her husband. "The roses are so beautiful. Thank you."

Christy's brother-in-law walked across the

room, and his eyes closed as he took his wife into his arms. He whispered something in her ear; Taylor smiled and nodded. The scene was an intimate one, and Christy felt like an intruder. She backed away, not looking at Cody until it was impossible to avoid him.

"Hello, again," he said. His voice was low and his smile contained a warmth and depth that multiplied a hundredfold all the sensations she'd experienced earlier, the very feelings she was trying to put out of her mind. Once again Christy was struck by the possessiveness she felt looking at him, studying him. For the past hour she'd been trying to understand why she should feel anything toward him. Nothing had come to her. No insights. Nothing.

They were barely more than strangers, and yet she felt completely comfortable with him. At the same time, he rattled her composure unlike anyone she'd ever met. It seemed absurdly ironic to be so flustered by a man and still feel so sheltered.

Cody glanced toward Russ and Taylor. "Would you like to go down to the nursery to view our godson?"

She nodded, gladly accepting an excuse to leave husband and wife alone.

Together she and Cody walked down the

familiar corridor until they stood in front of the large nursery window. But it wasn't the newborns that captured their attention. They made comments about little Eric and the other babies, but what interested them most was each other. After a while they gave up the pretense of looking at the newborns.

"Russ phoned the ranch and is having a couple of his hands drive a car over for him," Cody said after a while. "He's planning to spend the day with Taylor."

Once more Christy nodded. It seemed all she was capable of doing. Being this close to Cody felt like being trapped in a magnetic force field. It didn't matter how much she resisted, she was drawn to him.

With a determined effort, she diverted her attention to Eric again. The infant was sleeping, swaddled in a pale blue receiving blanket. A long-sleeved T-shirt covered his tiny arms and fists. He was so small, so adorable.

Cody's eyes followed hers, and when he spoke, his voice was filled with astonishment. "He's really something, isn't he?"

"Yes." Her voice was a whisper. "And to think we could've ended up delivering him."

"We?" Cody joked. "In all my years of law enforcement I've been spared that. Thank God."

Standing behind her, Cody's large hands held her shoulders, as if he'd been holding and touching her for a lifetime. It felt right and good to have this man so close. A small shudder skimmed down her spine at the innocent contact.

Cody must have noticed it, because he turned her around to face him, his eyes narrowing slightly. "You're trembling."

She couldn't deny it. This man she hardly knew confused her, bewildered her. The worst part was that she couldn't understand why. She'd met and dated any number of attractive, compelling men before. Yet none of them had ever overwhelmed her the way Cody did.

"Are you cold?"

"No," she answered quickly, flustered by his questions.

"What's wrong?"

How could she possibly explain something she couldn't grasp herself? "Nothing."

His eyes found hers, and she could've sworn they went several shades darker. "Does this happen often?"

"No." She shook her head. "Does it to you?" Christy swallowed, astonished she'd had the courage to ask him such a personal question.

"No," he answered after a moment.

"Never."

She pulled her gaze away, baffled by his openness. His honesty. It was exactly what she'd longed to hear. And what she'd feared.

"I . . . I need to get back to the ranch," she said, seeking an excuse to do something, anything to end this heightened awareness between them. "Taylor asked me to make some phone calls for her."

Cody lowered his eyes to her lips, his look, unhurried and sensual, as intimate as a kiss. Christy's stomach became a churning mass of doubts, mingled with an abundance of misgivings. She wanted to blame this feeling on the chaotic events of the day.

Slowly, almost unaware of what she was doing, Christy raised her own eyes to meet Cody's. He didn't look too comfortable. In fact, he seemed as perplexed and hesitant as she.

"I need to get back myself," he murmured.

Not until that moment did Christy realize the only way she had of returning to Cougar Point was with Cody. A sinking feeling assailed her. She couldn't possibly avoid an hour or more with him in the intimate confines of his vehicle.

Cody Franklin had no idea what was happening between him and his best friend's sister-in-law. To be honest, he hadn't paid Christy Manning much attention until they were in the hospital waiting room. She'd been terribly agitated, flipping through one magazine after another. Cody doubted she'd read a single word.

Then Russ had appeared and said that Taylor was ready for the delivery room, and Cody had watched as Christy started to completely unravel.

He'd suggested they take a short walk in an effort to help her relax. He didn't know how much comfort he'd be to her, since he was a stranger, but the least he could do was try. He knew from his years as a lawman that some physical activity might help take her mind off her sister.

It was when they'd stopped to look at the babies in the nursery that Cody had felt the faint stirring of something more. Faint stirring, hell, it was like a fist to his gut!

From that moment on, some emotion had started to awaken deep within him. He experienced a lost sensation, as if he were charting unknown land, and each turn led him farther away from all that was familiar. He was suddenly at a loss for words; he'd planned to involve her in conversation, occupy her with inane chitchat about Seattle and her job to keep her from thinking about

Taylor, but he hadn't asked a single question.

Every time Cody started to speak, he got lost in her eyes. He'd never seen a woman with eyes quite this blue. They reminded him of the coldest days of winter, when everything around him seemed to anticipate the promise of spring. When she smiled, those same blue eyes brightened even more, and it was like watching sunshine emerge after rain.

She'd look at him, and Cody swore he could see all the way to her soul. She was guileless and genuine and so lovely, it was all he could do not to stare at her, something he'd already apologized for once that day.

Twice he'd placed his hands on her shoulders. It wasn't his habit to comfort women with physical gestures, and he didn't understand his own actions. When he'd first held her, she'd obviously been shaken by Russ's news about Taylor, and he'd reached out in an effort to steady her.

The moment his hands had closed over her shoulders, his heart had begun racing like a runaway train. That hadn't happened since he was thirteen and had kissed a girl for the very first time.

Twenty-two years had passed, and the impact now was nearly as strong. Every

41

minute with her he learned something new about himself, and every emotion he discovered only bewildered him more.

"I'm sorry if it's an inconvenience for you to take me out to the ranch," Christy said, sliding into the front seat of his four-wheel drive.

"It isn't a problem." The only difficulty it created was of his own making. He was caught in some mysterious web of yearning. Perhaps, in some strange way, this all had to do with Russ and Taylor. He couldn't help envying the happiness his friends had found. Taylor was the best thing that had ever happened to Russ Palmer, and now Russ was a father.

Cody paused, half expecting to feel a twinge of jealousy or resentment. When he was introduced to Taylor a year ago, he'd wanted to date her himself, but she'd already met Russ and it was clear that she was falling in love with him. Cody had stood on the sidelines and watched their romance unfold, amused at the way they'd both fought it so hard.

No, jealousy hadn't prompted these feelings; he was convinced of that. His only reaction was happiness for his friends — a pure sense of shared joy.

The drive, which had seemed like four

hundred miles earlier in the day with Taylor and Russ in the backseat, went quickly on the return trip. Christy said little, but neither seemed uneasy with the silence. Occasionally Cody would look over at her, and their eyes would meet. Each time, some magic would pass involuntarily between them, some entrancement. After a while it became a challenge to discover what fascinated him about Taylor's sister, and he found his gaze repeatedly drawn to her as he attempted to analyze his attraction.

She was pretty, but no prettier than any number of women he'd dated. Not as beautiful as Becca. He paused, surprised that he didn't immediately feel a jolt of pain as he thought about her. It had been three years since Becca had turned his life upside down. He tried not to think of her at all, tried to ignore her memory as though he'd never known her at all. For the most part he succeeded . . . For the most part.

"Would you like to stop and get something to eat?" Cody asked as they neared Cougar Point. He wasn't hungry so much as reluctant to leave her.

He should've been exhausted. He'd had only a couple of hours sleep in the past forty-eight. Instead he felt alive. Reborn.

All he knew was that he'd met a woman, a

warm, caring, generous woman, and he felt as if his life was starting over again.

"I'm starved," Christy said enthusiastically. "I was so concerned about Taylor this morning that I forgot to eat breakfast."

"I haven't had anything, either."

"I got you out of bed when I phoned, didn't I?"

Cody nodded. Hell, he'd give his right hand to have her wake him every morning. "I worked the graveyard shift last night."

"You must be exhausted."

On the contrary, Cody had never felt more energetic. "Not at all," he said, mustering a smile to reassure her. "There are a couple of decent restaurants in town, but if you're interested in breakfast, the best place to eat is the bowling alley."

"Great."

Cody had expected her to laugh or to question his choice. She was, after all, a city girl, and he doubted that anyone in Seattle had ever taken her out to eat at a bowling alley. But she accepted his choice enthusiastically.

Since it was midafternoon by this time, the parking lot was nearly deserted. Christy didn't wait for him to come around and open the door for her, a fact that didn't surprise him. Taylor hadn't waited for him to open her door the one time he'd gone out with her, either.

Cody chose a booth toward the back of the restaurant and slid into the red vinyl seat. Christy sat across from him and reached for the menu, which was tucked between the sugar bowl and the salt and pepper shakers.

"Howdy, Cody," Mary Andrews said as she came over to the table, carrying two water glasses. She glanced curiously at Christy.

"This is Taylor's sister, Christy Manning. Christy, Mary Andrews."

"I don't suppose Taylor had her baby, did she?" Mary asked.

Christy's eyes softened as she nodded. "This morning. Eric Russell Palmer weighed in at eight pounds, three ounces."

Mary grinned from ear to ear. "That's terrific. You don't mind if I let folks know, do you?"

Christy shook her head. "Please do."

Still grinning, Mary pulled a small pad from her apron pocket. "What can I get for you two?"

"I'll have the breakfast special," Christy said, closing her menu. "With coffee."

"So will I," Cody said, sliding his own menu back into place.

Mary wrote down their order, then walked back to the kitchen.

For a long time Cody said nothing. Partly because he didn't know what to say and partly because he didn't feel the need to fill the silence with small talk. He was comfortable with Christy. He hadn't felt that way with any woman, ever. He looked over at her and wondered if she was experiencing this same sense of serenity, and instinctively knew she was. "What are you thinking?" he asked as Mary filled two cups with coffee.

Christy added cream to hers, took a sip and smiled. "If we're Eric's godparents, does that mean the two of us are related?"

A grin lit his face. "I suppose it does. I'm just not sure how."

"Me, neither."

One thing he did know: the idea of being linked to Christy pleased him immeasurably. "Tell me about yourself." He wanted to know everything there was to know about her from the time she was in preschool to the present.

"I'm the youngest of five."

"Spoiled?"

"Terribly."

He deliberately drew his gaze away from her mouth, which had fascinated him for several minutes. Beyond question, he knew

46

he was going to kiss her. He didn't know when. Soon, if possible. Nor did he know where. Only that it was quickly becoming an obsession.

"What about you?" Christy asked, pulling a napkin from the holder and spreading it across her lap, taking time to smooth it out. She seemed to be avoiding eye contact with him. That didn't surprise Cody. He'd been blatantly staring at her every chance he got. Her mouth enthralled him as nothing ever had. Soft. Pink. Moist. Just right for kissing.

"What about you?" she repeated, and the question seemed to echo.

"I was born in Miles City," he said, focusing on his coffee. "In the same hospital as Eric, as a matter of fact."

"Was your father a rancher?"

"No. He was a lawman, just as his father was before him. The Franklins have a long tradition of upholding law and order in Custer County."

"Did you always want to work for the sheriff's department?"

"Always. For as long as I can remember I dreamed of wearing a badge."

"They must be proud of you," she said in a way that made his heart quicken. What she was said was true. But his father and grandfather would never know he'd been

47

elected sheriff; his two younger sisters were the only family he had left.

Cody didn't want to talk about himself, not when there was so much to learn about her. "What did *you* want to be when you were a kid?"

"Not a paralegal," she said, then looked away, as if the words had slipped out before she could stop them. "I didn't even know what they were until high school. Sad to say, my dreams were far more traditional. I wanted to be a mommy."

"And now?"

"And now," she repeated in a whisper, frowning.

She was saved from having to answer by Mary, who brought two platters to their table. Each was heaped high with steaming hash browns, scrambled eggs, sausage and toast.

Their conversation ceased as they both picked up their forks. Neither spoke for several minutes.

"I didn't realize how hungry I was," Christy said, reaching for the small container of jam. She peeled back the cover and scooped out the preserves with her knife.

"Where's Mandy?" Cody asked, remembering Russ's teenage sister, who lived with Russ and Taylor, for the first time that day.

"She's with a friend. Russ phoned from the hospital and told her about Eric. She had lots of questions and was sorry she missed all the excitement."

Cody pushed his empty plate aside. Mary stopped by the table to refill their coffee mugs and take away Cody's plate.

"You might as well take mine, too," Christy said, leaning back in the booth. She placed her hands over her flat stomach and sighed. "I can't believe I ate all that."

"Can I get you anything else?" Mary asked.

"Nothing, thanks," Cody answered for them.

Mary set the bill on the table and walked away with a quick backward wave.

They left the restaurant a few minutes later. Cody opened the door for Christy, insisting on the courtesy because he enjoyed doing something, however small, for her.

She seemed preoccupied and anxious on the ride to the Lazy P. He started to ask her how long she planned to stay, but even before he'd finished the question, he knew she wasn't listening.

"I'm sorry. What did you say?" she asked, glancing at him.

"It wasn't important." He pulled off the main road and headed down the long, dusty driveway. This time of year the road was filled with ruts deep enough to send them both bouncing around the interior of his Cherokee if he wasn't careful to watch where he was driving. In several spots he slowed down to ten or so miles an hour. Then he was forced to ask himself if it was his car he was concerned about — or the fact that the sooner he arrived at the ranch, the sooner he'd have to leave Christy.

Once he reached the ranch yard, he turned off the engine and climbed out of the cab. Christy had opened the car door, offering him just the excuse he needed to touch her. His hands slid around her slim waist and he lifted her down.

She hadn't been expecting his help and, caught off guard, she fell forward. She made a small sound as her hands came into contact with his chest.

Neither moved. Cody couldn't believe how good it felt to have her in his arms again.

"I'm sorry," she whispered.

"I'm not." Cody had never been one to beat around the bush, as the saying went. "Not in the least," he added.

Her hands were against his chest, and he wondered if she could feel how fast his heart was beating, wondered if she had even an inkling of what he was feeling.

"Thanks for breakfast and the ride home," she murmured, but made no effort to move away from him.

Heat radiated from where her hands were touching him, warming him in ways he couldn't understand but didn't question. She tensed her fingers as if to pull away, but if that was her intention, she didn't follow through.

Cody raised his hand to the side of her neck. His fingers stroked the kitten-soft skin there, and he watched, fascinated, as she slowly closed her eyes.

Once more his gaze sought her mouth. Her lush, vulnerable mouth. Never had it looked more inviting than it did at that moment.

It seemed only natural to kiss her. Hell, he'd been thinking about doing exactly that for hours, but now that the opportunity presented itself, he hesitated. It was as if an inborn defense mechanism flashed a warning through his system. Kiss Christy Manning and you'll never be the same again, it seemed to be saying.

But the words of caution counted for nothing. Cody couldn't have stopped himself if he'd wanted to. Whatever came after, whatever life held for him, whatever the cost, he was going to kiss this woman.

Unhurriedly, deliberately, he pressed his lips over hers. She murmured something, Cody didn't know what, and he felt the movement against his mouth.

Her lips were everything Cody had dreamed they would be. Warm. Moist. Devastating. With a whimper she responded immediately. It was as if he'd never kissed a woman before this moment.

Her arms made their way around his neck as she leaned into him. Her softness melded into his hardness, and white-hot sensation seemed to explode inside him. Cody kissed her again and again, his hands in her hair, cradling the back of her head. He kissed her until his breathing became labored. Until he heard her moan, and then realized it was his own sigh of longing that echoed in his ears. Still he didn't release her. He held her against him, never wanting to let her go.

Only when Christy stiffened did Cody slacken his hold. Slowly he opened his eyes to discover her looking up at him, her beautiful eyes bright with tears. He frowned because he didn't understand. Then, in a heartbeat, he did. The kissing had affected her as profoundly as it had him.

"I know what you're thinking," he whispered, lifting her chin with his finger, dropping his mouth to hers, unable to resist.

"You don't," she said. "You couldn't possibly know."

"But I do," he countered. "You're thinking this is the craziest thing that's ever happened to you. I know because that's exactly what I'm thinking. We just met this morning, and yet I feel I've known you all my life."

Her eyes widened as if his words had hit their mark.

"All of this is because of Taylor and Russ," she told him. "Their happiness, their excitement must be rubbing off on us. Don't you see how foolish this is?"

"No." He didn't mean to be blunt or obtuse. He was nearly thirty-five years old and long past the age of playing games. Christy was younger, but she knew, the same way he did. She might choose to deny it, but he wouldn't.

"Are you saying you didn't want me to kiss you?" he asked, trusting her to be honest, because he didn't believe she could be anything else.

It took her a minute to answer him, and when she did her voice was raspy. "That's the problem. . . . I've never wanted anything more."

THREE

Christy woke early the next morning after a restless night's sleep. She'd tossed and turned so frequently that the sheets had been pulled loose from the bed and the bedspread had slipped onto the floor. Staring up at the ceiling, Christy slowly expelled her breath while mulling over the events of the day before.

So much had happened.

Taylor's son had been born, and Christy had been introduced to the newly elected sheriff of Custer County.

However, Christy had more than *met* Cody Franklin. He'd taken her to breakfast late in the afternoon, and when he dropped her off at the ranch, he'd kissed her — and she'd let him. More than *let* him; she'd encouraged him. What she'd told him was true. She'd never wanted anyone's kiss more.

Admitting as much certainly wasn't one

of her more intelligent moves, but then it hadn't been her mind doing the talking. It had been her heart.

Once again she tried to focus her thoughts on James. He'd been so sweet the evening he'd given her the engagement ring. They'd gone out for dinner, sitting at the table with candlelight flickering and soft music playing in the background. Christy had noticed that he'd barely touched his meal. He seemed nervous, then started talking nonstop. Normally James was a calm, quiet man, not easily agitated. He'd been rambling for about fifteen minutes, and Christy couldn't figure out where the discussion was leading. She'd told him so. Then James had gotten flustered.

Before Christy could react, James pulled a ring box from the inside of his suit pocket. He'd been so endearing, so wonderfully sweet as he held out the diamond, letting the ring speak for him.

By then Christy had become so flustered herself that all she could do was stare at the lovely solitary diamond glittering up at her. James had withdrawn it from its velvet bed, and without a word she'd given him her hand.

The entire thing hadn't taken more than a few seconds. She'd promised to become his wife, promised to pledge her life to him without a word of love spoken between them. James cared for her, Christy felt assured of it. He wouldn't have offered her the ring if he didn't. By the same token, she loved him. Otherwise she wouldn't have accepted his proposal.

Afterward, James had been ecstatic as he'd hugged and kissed her. The ring was too large and had nearly slipped off her finger as she'd shown it to her parents that same night. Both Eric and Elizabeth Manning had been thrilled with the news of Christy's engagement to the up-and-coming attorney.

It wasn't until two days later, just before she left for Montana, that the first of the doubts had come. She loved James, she reminded herself, repeating it again and again on the endless drive across three states.

James was a good man. He'd been a friend long before they'd become romantically involved, and judging by everything she'd read, friends made the best husbands.

Perhaps the most convincing argument for this marriage was how comfortable Christy felt with him. Her parents thought the world of James; in fact, they seemed more excited than she was about the prospect of his joining the family. Her father talked of little else, promising Christy the wedding of the year.

But if she'd been experiencing a few niggling doubts before she left Seattle, they'd multiplied a hundredfold since she'd arrived in Montana and met Cody Franklin.

Cody.

For more reasons than she dared explore, she struggled to push every thought of the sheriff from her mind.

With a determination born of pride and a sense of fairness and truth that had been ingrained in her from birth, Christy decided to tell Russ, tell someone, anyone, about her engagement. She climbed out of bed and got dressed, then went in seach of her brother-in-law.

Russ, however, had already left the house. A note was propped against the sugar bowl, explaining he'd be with his men that morning, and she shouldn't look for him before noon. He also wrote that he wouldn't be able to visit Taylor and the baby until that evening. He signed his name, adding that Christy should make herself at home.

Defeat settled over Christy. She couldn't keep quiet about herself and James much longer and still hold her head high.

It took only an hour to straighten up the house. She cooked herself some eggs, then realized she wasn't hungry. Russ, on the other hand, had apparently fixed himself a breakfast large enough to feed five men. He'd made a minimal effort to clean the kitchen; clearly, he'd been in a rush.

With time to spare, Christy wandered outside, wanting to investigate what she could of the grounds. Since Russ was visiting Taylor that evening, she'd drive to the hospital in the afternoon.

One hand leading a chestnut horse paused and stared at her when she appeared.

"Good morning," Christy said cheerfully.

"Howdy." The lanky cowboy straightened and touched the rim of his hat. He looped the reins around a fencepost, then walked toward her. A fistful of cigars with pale blue bands was sticking out of his shirt pocket, evidence of Russ's eagerness to spread the news of his son's birth.

"You must be part of Mrs. Palmer's family."

"Christy Manning," she said, holding out her hand. "I'm Taylor's sister."

The middle-aged man took pains to remove his thick leather glove and clasped her soft palm in his callused one. "Pleased to make your acquaintance. Russ is out this morning, but I s'pect he'll be back soon. Most folks call me Billy Joe."

"Good to meet you, Billy Joe," Christy said, looking toward the barn. Several horses stuck their sleek heads over the stall doors, glancing at her with open curiosity.

"If you'll excuse me," Billy Joe said, backing away from her. His horse was saddled and waiting, prancing in place. "This gelding's anxious to be on his way."

"Of course. I'm sorry. I didn't mean to hold you up."

"No problem." He mounted the gelding in a single smooth motion. Pulling back on the reins, Billy Joe nodded at her once more, then galloped out of the yard.

Left to her own devices, Christy wandered toward the barn, stopping in front of the first stall. The name Shadow was burned into a wood plaque above the door.

"Howdy, Shadow," Christy said. "You look like a friendly horse." Friendly enough, at any rate, for her to venture petting his nose. She stroked it a few times while the gelding took pride in revealing his teeth and nickered his approval.

Seeing a large barrel of grain near the middle of the barn, Christy stepped over to it, intending to reach for a handful of oats. She didn't know much about horses, but figured a handful of oats would win approval.

"I thought I might find you in here," a deep male voice said from the barn door.

Christy's heart shot to her throat. Cody. She turned to see him silhouetted against the morning sunlight. Tall, lean and dark. He wore jeans and a western shirt with a string tie and was so strikingly handsome that for a moment all she could do was stare.

"Hello," she said, returning to her task, her hands trembling. It wasn't fair that he should have this effect on her. But then, she was learning that little in life was fair.

Her hand loaded with grain, she walked back to Shadow's stall.

"Be sure to feed that to him with your palm flat, otherwise he might inadvertently bite you," Cody warned, moving toward her.

Christy was grateful for the advice and did as he suggested. Shadow ate the oats quickly, and when he'd finished, Christy wiped her hand on her jeans. Her heart was hammering so hard, she was certain Cody could hear it.

"Did you sleep well?"

"No," she answered honestly. Her back was to him, but that didn't help. She felt warm and dizzy just knowing he was there.

"I couldn't, either." His voice was soft and raspy. Sensual. "I only had a couple of hours of sleep the night before, so I should've nodded off the minute my head touched the pillow. But I didn't. I couldn't."

Christy found a strange comfort in knowing his sleep had been as unsettled as her own. "I . . . tossed and turned most of the night, then finally drifted off toward morning."

"Me, too."

When he'd left her the night before, she'd stood inside the house and watched him drive away, feeling restless and uneasy. That disquiet hadn't dissipated until the moment he'd stepped into the barn. Cody spoke, and instantly the emptiness had started to leave her, as if a sense of order had been restored to her life.

Except that it wasn't right. Everything was very, very wrong.

"We need to talk."

"Yes," she whispered. She'd meant to tell Russ about James, knowing her brother-in-law would mention the fact to Cody. But this was better. She could tell Cody herself. Explain before either of them got hurt. Before things went too far.

Honesty really was the best policy. She'd grown up believing that. Practicing it.

Christy was searching for just the right words, irritated with herself for not having thought this out beforehand. There should be an easy way to say it. The truth shouldn't be this difficult.

Then Cody was behind her, so close she could feel the heat radiating from his body. His hands settled over her shoulders, his touch light and warm and reassuring. Slowly he turned her around so she faced him.

Their eyes locked, and Christy's throat went tight. His were beautiful, as dark and rich as the finest coffee. They were the eyes of a man who'd only recently learned to dream. Wistful eyes. Pensive eyes.

"Every time I'd try to sleep, all I could think about was you." His tone said that he'd struggled long and hard against allowing her to dominate his thoughts.

"It was the same with me." She shouldn't have told him that. Shouldn't admit his effect on her in one breath and then tell him about James in the next. "But I —"

"I couldn't stop thinking about how good you felt in my arms."

She knew exactly what he was saying because she'd experienced the same thing herself. He felt good to her, too, the kind of good that made everything feel right even when it was wrong. The kind of good that never diminished, never ceased.

"You felt it, didn't you?" He seemed to need confirmation from her.

She gave it reluctantly, breathlessly, lowering her eyes. "Yes."

They lapsed into silence then, as though neither of them knew what else to say. There didn't seem to be any need for words. Christy understood what Cody was thinking and feeling as clearly as if he'd spoken.

I need to kiss you again and discover if last night was real. He asked her with his eyes.

No, her heart cried. She couldn't allow it. If Cody kissed her again, she'd be forced to confront issues she dared not face. Cody Franklin was a stranger. James was her fiancé. Her friend.

I've frightened you.

No, came the cry from the farthest corner of her heart. *Yes,* she countered immediately. Cody stirred emotions she didn't know she was capable of feeling. Emotions she'd never experienced with any man. Each time they were together, her awareness of him became more intense. This shouldn't be happening to her. Not now. Not *ever.* She was engaged to another man.

Frowning, Cody took one step toward her. Christy's heart surged.

Don't, please, don't, she pleaded silently. *I can't refuse you. I can't refuse myself.*

But Cody had apparently given up listening to the cries of her heart. When she

63

looked at him, he was both watchful and silent.

Before another second could pass, he reached for her, and whatever resistance she'd been able to muster burst like the white filaments of a dandelion in the wind. His mouth found hers, smooth and firm against her softness. She moaned in protest, but her small cry soon became a sigh of welcome, of need, of pleasure.

A tenderness blossomed within her, the sensations so exquisite they shocked her even more than they had a day earlier. It shouldn't be this good, this wonderful, she told herself over and over, wanting to weep with frustration. Yet it was better than anything she'd ever experienced.

Cody continued to kiss her with a passion and an excitement that left Christy clinging to him.

"I can't believe this," he murmured, and her mind echoed his words. She was struggling with reality, and felt lost and weak.

Cody bent his head and dropped a succession of kisses down her neck and along her jaw until she moaned. He responded with a small, throaty sound and quickly joined their mouths again, kissing hers softly.

Christy went weak with need. She was

melting from the heat. Burning up with fever. Consumed with a sweet warmth that threatened to devour her. "No," she whimpered. "We can't do . . . this."

Cody raised his hands and held them against the sides of her face.

He was going too fast for her. Her own body was going too fast for her. She felt as though she were sitting on a runaway horse, galloping out of control, being propelled farther and farther away from reason.

"I feel as if I've been waiting for you all my life," Cody whispered, wrapping his arms completely around her. His hand reached up to smooth the hair from her temple. "I can only imagine what you must think of me coming here like this."

Her eyes remained closed, and her dark world continued to spin without restraint. Even when she opened her eyes, everything was blurred and out of focus, her thoughts hopelessly addled.

"I didn't mean to shock you," he said.

"You didn't. I shocked myself."

Cody worked his thumbs sensuously across the high curve of her cheekbones. He frowned as he felt her tears. "I hurt you?"

"No . . ." she murmured, looking away. Now she understood the restless feeling she'd experienced all night. She'd been haunted by his kiss, haunted by the emotions and the need he'd created within her.

All of this had to stop. Now. This instant. She pressed her forehead against his solid chest, needing his strength in order to find the courage to say what she had to say.

His hand lifted her hair, his touch gentle as though fingering strands of silk.

"I fall apart when you kiss me," she confessed.

His throaty laugh was filled with amusement and tenderness. "*You* fall apart?" He captured her hand and pressed it over his heart. "See what you do to me?"

She didn't need to touch him to realize how his pulse was churning beneath her palm. Unable to watch the disillusionment in his eyes when she told him about James, she closed her own.

"I've never felt anything for anyone as strongly as I have for you," she said softly. Then she didn't say anything more for a long moment, carefully formulating her words.

Cody obviously sensed that she felt troubled because he tucked his finger under her chin and raised her head. His gaze caressed her. "Christy?"

"Please listen," she whispered, her voice trembling. "There's something you should know, something I meant to tell you from the first, only —"

"Cody, what are you doing here?" Russ's voice echoed through the barn like thunder. "Everything's all right with Taylor, isn't it?" Christy's brother-in-law stopped abruptly when he saw Cody's arms around her waist. He removed his Stetson and wiped his forehead with the back of his hand. "I wasn't interrupting anything, was I?"

"Your timing couldn't be worse," Cody barked, glaring at his friend.

Russ didn't appear the least bit concerned. He tossed a load of baling wire into his pickup and promptly reached for another. If anything, he looked amused.

"This isn't funny."

Russ paused. "Now that's where I disagree. You just met Christy. Until yesterday you hadn't so much as set eyes on her. I don't mind telling you, Franklin, I've never known you to work so fast."

"Shut your fool mouth before you say something I'll make you regret," Cody grumbled. His threat wasn't worth a dime and Russ knew it, but he felt he had to respond.

"She is a pretty little thing, isn't she?" Another wheel of wire landed on top of the first with a loud, discordant clang. He turned to stare at Cody when he didn't answer right away. "Isn't she?" he repeated.

"Yes," Cody admitted grudgingly.

"For a moment there, it looked like the two of you had been kissing." Once more Russ paused, a grin turning up the edges of his mouth.

"I *was* kissing her," Cody said, challenging Russ to make something of the fact if he wanted to. He was as uncomfortable as he could ever remember being with his friend. Russ was curious to learn what was going on between him and Christy, but unfortunately Cody could think of no way of explaining his feelings for Christy, especially with the mood Russ was in. His friend seemed to find the situation downright comical.

"I guessed as much." Russ wiped the sweat from his brow, but Cody had a sneaking suspicion that he did so to cover a smile. Not that Russ had any trouble poking fun at him and letting him know it.

After Russ arrived, and the three of them had exchanged pleasantries, Christy excused herself and left, saying that she was driving to Miles City to visit Taylor and Eric. Cody would have offered to go with her, but he was working swing shift and it wasn't likely that he'd be back before he was scheduled to go on duty.

"You're not going to get closemouthed with me now, are you?" Russ was asking. "I can't say I've ever seen you take to a woman the way you have to Taylor's sister. What's different about Christy?"

"What was different about Taylor?"

Russ chuckled. "Touché. But if you remember correctly, all Taylor and I could do at first was argue. Never met a woman who could irritate me as much as she did."

"You didn't stay angry at her for long."

Russ shook his head. "No, can't say I did. She'd make me so furious I couldn't think straight. Before I could stop myself, I'd say or do some fool thing I'd end up regretting. That certainly doesn't seem to be the case with you and Christy, though. You two can't seem to keep your hands off each other."

Cody decided it was best to ignore that comment. "You and Taylor worked things out, and that's what matters."

Some of the humor disappeared from Russ's dark eyes. "We did, didn't we?" A faraway expression came over him. "Did you get a good look at him, Cody?"

Before Cody could respond Russ continued. "The nurse handed me Eric, and I swear something happened to my heart. It was the craziest thing, holding that baby in my arms and loving him so much my throat got all clogged up. I couldn't have said a word if my life depended on it. Before I knew what was happening, tears were rolling down my face. *Me.* I can't remember the last time I cried. I've never felt anything as incredible as holding my son.

"You know, I loved Taylor before the baby was born, but it pales in comparison to what I felt for her as she struggled to give birth to Eric. I've always thought of women as the weaker sex, but I was wrong." He shook himself as if waking from a deep sleep, his eyes as somber as Cody had ever seen.

"You have reason to be proud."

"I bought every box of cigars the gift shop owned."

"I know. I was with you."

"Hell, I don't even smoke."

Cody laughed. "I know that, too." He hesitated, uncertain how to proceed. "About Christy . . . You don't have any objection to my seeing her, do you?"

"So you plan to take her to Sitting Bull Lookout?" The ridge above the town had been their favorite necking place as teenagers.

"Probably," Cody answered, trying to hold back a grin.

Russ tucked his hands in his hip pockets. "Then you really are serious?"

"I've never been more serious in my life," Cody admitted without a pause.

Taylor was sound asleep when Christy got to the hospital. Her sister's long hair spread out over the white pillows like spilled coffee. Her eyes were closed, her breathing deep and even.

Tiptoeing into the room so as not to disturb her, Christy pulled out the lone chair and sat. Although she'd been on the road for more than an hour, she remained as upset and nervous as when she'd left the house.

She felt like weeping. She felt like rejoicing. No woman should experience such conflicting emotions.

The obedient, do-what's-right-at-all-costs part of her kept reminding her of James. Loyal, hardworking James, who loved her.

All her life Christy had done what was right. She'd never been rebellious. She'd been a model child. A model sister. Respectful. Considerate. Thoughtful.

She felt none of those things now.

The look Cody had given her just before Russ stepped into the barn would be forever burned in her mind. It was the kind of look a woman dreams of receiving from a man sometime in her life. A lover's look. One so intimate and personal that it could never be explained to another.

If this intense feeling between her and Cody was wrong, then why did Christy feel so good inside? Why did she long to throw up her arms and shout for joy? If this was being rebellious or disrespectful, then all Christy could say was that she was entering puberty later than the normal teenager. About ten years later.

Taylor stirred and opened her eyes. "Christy," she said, yawning. "When did you arrive?"

"About five minutes ago."

"You should have woken me."

"And interrupted your nap?" she teased. "How are you feeling?"

"Wonderful." A soft smile touched her eyes. "Eric spent most of the morning with me. Oh, Christy, he's so adorable. We became acquainted with each other. I counted his fingers and toes, and he taught me about breast feeding."

"You look happy."

"I am . . . I really am."

Christy settled farther down in the chair. Trying not to be obvious, she stared at the floor, studying the pattern in the white tile.

"Cody took me out to eat when we left here yesterday."

"In Miles City?"

"No. We went to the bowling alley in Cougar Point."

"I'm glad." There was a pause. "He's a good man."

Christy knew that instinctively. "I thought so, too. I like him, Taylor. I really do."

"Why do you look so guilty?"

How could she look or feel anything else? But Taylor wouldn't understand. Her sister had no way of knowing about the lovely engagement ring being sized at the Seattle jewelers.

They chatted for a few minutes before Taylor settled back against the pillows and sighed.

"What was that all about?"

"What?"

"That sigh," Christy said.

"Oh . . . I was just thinking about you and Cody. I'm really pleased you like him so much. Frankly, I've been concerned about you seeing so much of James."

Christy was surprised she didn't give everything away right then and there. "Oh?" she managed.

"He's nice, don't get me wrong, but he's so boring. To be honest, I've never understood what you saw in him."

"But he's kind."

"So is Big Bird!" Taylor argued. "I think James is a nice guy, but he isn't the right one for you, and I can't understand why you continue to date him."

"How can you say that?" Christy demanded, forcing the argument. James had been a child prodigy, a recognized genius by age ten. He graduated from high school in his early teens, and from law school at twenty. At twenty-five he was close to becoming the youngest partner in Atwater and Beckham's long, distinguished history. "James is a a really nice man."

"True," Taylor agreed readily enough. "But he isn't the right one for you," she said again.

"You're wrong." A simple way to end this argument would be for Christy to announce her engagement, yet she hesitated, interested in hearing her sister's opinion.

"James is everything you say, but you're not in love with him and never have been," Taylor announced with a challenging smile.

"You sound so confident of that."

"I am. You couldn't possibly be in love with James if you're this interested in Cody Franklin."

Any objection Christy might have posed

died a quick and quiet death.

"I think," Taylor said, holding out her hands to her sister, "you came to Montana at exactly the right time."

FOUR

"Can I hold Eric?" Mandy Palmer asked minutes after Taylor was home from the hospital. "I barely got a chance to look at him before," she added, casting an accusing glance in the direction of her older brother.

"Of course," Taylor said, leading the teenager into the living room. Russ followed, leaving Christy standing alone in the kitchen with Cody.

She busied herself at the stove, praying the sheriff would go with the others.

He didn't.

"You've been avoiding me," he said softly, leaning against the kitchen counter and crossing his arms over his chest. It was all Christy could do not to stare at him. If she did, he'd be able to read the longing in her eyes, and he'd realize she'd been miserable and unhappy and at odds with herself.

She'd needed these two days to think. To come to grips with herself. To decide.

The answers hadn't come easily. She'd wrestled with the most momentous decision of her life. The resolution had come, but not without a price. She felt exhausted, frightened and on the verge of tears.

She couldn't deny Cody's words. She *had* been avoiding him. She'd astonished herself at how clever she'd been about it. Clever enough so no one would have guessed.

Except Cody.

"Why didn't you answer my calls?" he asked.

"I came to spend time with Taylor, to help her. I've been busy. . . ."

No one had bothered to tell her that Cody had been invited to Taylor and Eric's welcome-home dinner. She wasn't prepared for this.

From the way everyone had disappeared the minute Taylor arrived, Christy shouldn't be surprised to find herself alone with Cody. It seemed as if it had all been prearranged.

"Christy, talk to me," he pleaded, his frustration evident. "Tell me what's wrong."

"Nothing. It's just that I've been so terribly busy." So terribly confused. So terribly guilty. Cowardly, too, since she'd been juggling with her conscience, her scruples and her sense of fairness.

If anything, this time away from Cody had

enlightened her. The first day she'd been trapped in the restless, lost sensation she'd experienced the night before, after he'd left.

The second day, however, she'd found peace. It was a strained peace and would be so until she went home to Seattle and talked to James. Nevertheless, she'd reached a decision.

For a good part of the afternoon, Mandy and Christy had worked together to get the house ready for Taylor's return with Eric. No one had said Cody would be returning with them.

No one had given her a word of warning. She didn't know what to say to him just now, and the truth seemed unwieldy. Awkward.

"I don't blame you if you're frightened," Cody continued, his voice low. "I'm frightened myself. The first time we kissed I felt like I'd been hit by a freight train. The second time it was even more powerful. . . . Deep down I'd hoped it was somehow tied up in the emotion surrounding Russ, Taylor and the baby, but it isn't."

"I don't think it is, either."

"If you're looking for an explanation of what's going on between us, I can't give you one. All I know is what I feel."

Sometimes, Christy believed, a lifetime of

doing the right thing could be subverted by pure sensation. This had certainly proved true with her and Cody.

"Talk to me."

Slowly she turned, witnessing for herself the tenderness, and the confusion, in his eyes. Without uttering a word, she walked over to him and slipped her arms around his waist. He placed his own around her, anchoring her to his chest as he expelled a harsh breath.

"Can you tell me what's troubling you?"

She nodded, almost giddy with relief and release. Raising her head, she smiled up at him, longing to reassure him. Part of her yearned to put this behind them and blurt it all out. She wanted to tell him about James and the engagement and how meeting him had turned her world inside out. But there wasn't enough time to untangle this mess before dinner. They needed privacy to discuss it in detail, time to reach an understanding.

She glanced regretfully toward the living room.

"Do you want to steal away?" Cody asked. "Go somewhere else?"

That was exactly what she did want, but they couldn't leave. Tonight was an evening to celebrate. Taylor and Eric were home for the first time, and leaving would be selfish and thoughtless.

"Forget I asked that," Cody murmured. "I'll be patient."

"So will I. We'll make some excuse after dinner," she suggested, then on impulse lightly brushed her lips over his.

Cody, however, wanted more. Much more. Placing his hands on each side of her neck, he pulled her tighter to him and wove his fingers through her short hair as he brought his mouth to hers.

"I swear," Russ exclaimed loudly, walking into the kitchen, "I can't leave these two alone for a moment." The words were followed by the sound of his laughter.

Languidly Cody eased his mouth from Christy's and slowly opened his eyes. "How about getting lost for the next few minutes?" Cody said.

"Fine with me," Russ agreed, "but I don't think that fried chicken's going to want to wait much longer."

"Oh, my," Christy said, abruptly breaking away. She'd completely forgotten about the dinner she and Mandy had so carefully planned. She grabbed a pot holder and moved the grease-spitting skillet from the burner. Heaving a sigh of relief, she brushed her bangs off her forehead.

"Need any help?" Mandy asked, sauntering into the kitchen. Russ's teenage sister lived with him and Taylor, and from everything Christy had heard, Mandy was the one responsible for bringing Russ and Taylor together. Because of a summer job and other commitments, Mandy had been away from the house during most of Christy's visit and Christy was only beginning to get to know her. And like her.

"No. I've got everything under control here."

Russ contradicted her under his breath, but Christy chose to ignore her brother-in-law's comment. She was relieved when the two men vacated the kitchen.

With Mandy's assistance, dinner was ready fifteen minutes later. Mandy called everyone, and they gathered around the dining room table. Russ escorted his wife, his eyes tender as he seated her.

Taylor, wearing a loose pale blue dress that complemented her eye color, looked wonderful. Every woman should look so good three days after giving birth, Christy mused.

"Oh, Christy . . . Mandy," Taylor said, studying the table. "This is fantastic. You must've spent the whole day cooking — and in this heat!"

"It wasn't a problem," Christy said automatically.

"Yes, it was," Mandy countered smoothly. "It took all afternoon, but we had so much fun it was worth it. Your sister's great!"

"I think so, too, but you shouldn't have gone to so much trouble." Taylor gestured at the three different kinds of salads, the platter of fried chicken and two separate desserts.

"But we did," Mandy said, reaching for the potato salad, "so you might as well enjoy it."

Christy shared a secret smile with her older sister. She admired Mandy for her openness and her honesty. Had she answered, she would've quickly allowed Taylor and the others to believe she'd managed to whip up a three-course meal in a matter of minutes without the slightest trouble.

Eric stirred just as they were finishing dinner, and Taylor immediately started to rise. Russ put his hand on her arm, stopping her.

"Let me?" He made it a question.

"He probably needs his diaper changed," Taylor warned.

"So? I can do it. Just how difficult can changing a diaper be?"

Christy and Taylor exchanged a meaningful glance. When she pulled her gaze away from her sister, Christy's eyes sought out Cody. The sheriff gave her a look of exaggerated shock.

"Did I hear correctly?" he teased. "Did Russ Palmer volunteer to change a diaper?"

"Apparently so," Taylor said, pretending to be as awed as Cody.

"All right, you guys, cut it out," Russ warned, shouting from the master bedroom.

"I don't know if I can let a moment like this pass without witnessing it myself. Does anyone have a camera?"

"You're not taking any damn picture," Russ roared, his voice booming through the house. His words were quickly followed by the squalling cry of an infant. A fraction of a second later Russ shouted for Taylor.

Christy tossed her napkin aside and left the table with her sister, wondering if she could help. Mandy was the only one content to let the others deal with the baby while she finished her meal.

The three of them crowded around the bassinet where Russ struggled with the diaper and pins. He was grumbling, and his face was creased with a deep frown as if he were performing major surgery.

"I marry the most modern woman in the world. She won't let me open a car door for her, insists on paying for her own dinner when we go out on a date, but will she use disposable diapers? Oh, no, she's got to torment me with cloth ones."

"They're better for the environment," Taylor said, gently pushing her husband aside. She dealt efficiently with the diaper-changing, completely unfazed by the task.

"That's all there is to it?" Cody asked, making fun of his friend's inability to handle such an uncomplicated situation.

"If you think it's so easy, you try it."

"I will, but probably not for several years." Cody looked at Christy, and the mental image of Cody holding a baby in his arms, their baby, filled her mind. She looked away, not wanting anyone to witness the emotion she was feeling.

Russ watched as Taylor lifted the dirty diaper from the bassinet. "What are you going to do with that . . . thing?" He wrinkled his nose as he asked the question.

"I'm putting it in the diaper pail in the bathroom."

"You're not keeping those smelly diapers in there, are you?" he said as he followed Taylor down the hallway. Christy could hear him listing his objections.

Once more Christy and Cody were left alone, this time with Eric. The infant lay on his back, squinting his blue eyes as he gazed up at them. His mouth made small sucking motions.

Unable to resist, Christy reached into the bassinet and lifted Eric out. He gurgled contentedly in her arms as she sat on the end of the bed. Cody stood next to her, studying the newborn. He lovingly smoothed his large hand along the side of the baby's head. Eric's tiny hand closed around Cody's index finger.

"Look," Cody said excitedly, as if Eric had broken an Olympic record. "I think he recognizes us."

"And well he should! We're his godparents," Christy reminded him. She turned to smile at Cody and once more found herself lost in his eyes.

In that brief moment Christy saw a reflection of everything she was feeling. Until now, whenever they looked at each other, their eyes brimmed with questions and doubts.

But this time was different. Christy saw in Cody an understanding. They'd each lost the need for answers or explanations.

"How long will you be in Cougar Point?" Cody asked.

"My vacation is two weeks."

Both seemed to calculate the number of

days remaining before she'd need to go home.

Cody's expression told her he wanted to spend every available moment he could with her. It was what Christy wanted, too, more than she'd wanted anything in her life.

"I'm working day shift tomorrow," he told her softly, his look tender. "What about dinner?"

"I'd like that." Which was definitely an understatement.

The air between them seemed to spark with sensuality. Cody leaned toward her, and Christy knew beyond a doubt that he intended to kiss her. He hesitated a fraction of an inch from her mouth before regretfully backing away.

"I'd bet my last dollar if I kissed you, Russ would interrupt us."

"He probably would. He seems to have an incredible sense of timing, doesn't he?"

As soon as she spoke, her brother-in-law stuck his head in the doorway. "What's taking you two so long? Mandy's got the coffee poured."

"See what I mean?" Cody whispered.

Christy nodded and stood, placing Eric over her shoulder and rubbing his back. He was so tiny, so perfect, and her heart swelled anew with love for him.

Taylor and Russ were sitting in the living room when Cody and Christy appeared. Their looks were openly curious — as if they were waiting for the couple to make an announcement.

Christy didn't think it would do much good to try to disguise what was going on between her and Cody. Her sister knew her far too well, and clearly Russ was equally familiar with Cody.

Christy handed the baby over to Taylor, dropping a kiss on his forehead as she did. By tacit agreement, she and Cody sat at opposite sides of the room. Being close to each other only intensified the attraction, and no doubt the curiosity.

"So," Russ said, glancing from Cody to Christy, sporting a wide grin.

"Russ," Taylor warned in a low whisper.

"What?"

"Do you have to be so obvious?"

Russ blinked, apparently at a loss to understand his wife's censure. "I didn't say anything, but if I did venture to mention the obvious, I'd say something along the lines of how happy I am that my best friend and your sister have apparently hit it off so well."

"To tell you the truth, I couldn't be more pleased myself," Taylor added, smiling.

Cody crossed his legs and picked up his coffee. "I'm glad to hear Christy and I have made you two so happy."

Russ chuckled at that, amusement glistening in his eyes. "Do you remember that time in the sixth grade?" Russ asked.

"I'm not likely to forget it."

"What are you two mumbling about now?" Taylor demanded.

"We were eleven."

"You were eleven," Cody corrected. "I was ten."

"Right," Russ agreed. "We'd been good friends for several years and had started to notice some of our other buddies turning traitor."

"Turning traitor?" Christy repeated.

"Liking girls."

Since Christy was the youngest of the five Manning children, she couldn't recall her brothers sharing similar feelings. "What did you two do?" she asked.

"The only thing we could," Russ explained, grinning again. "We were losing our best friends left and right, so Cody and I made a pact and became blood brothers. We made a solemn vow never to associate with any of the guys who'd turned traitor and liked girls."

"Especially pretty ones with dark hair and

bright blue eyes," Cody remarked, looking at Christy, who possessed both. His mouth quivered, and she realized he was only a breath away from laughing outright.

"And which of you broke this sacred vow first?"

"Cody did," Russ said.

"Russ," Cody responded, the two speaking almost simultaneously.

"Boys, please," Taylor said in what Christy was sure was her best schoolteacher voice.

"Cody gave Mary Lu Hawkins a valentine that year," Russ reminded him.

"My mother forced me to do it," Cody insisted. "I never liked Mary Lu Hawkins, and you know it."

"That's not what I heard."

Listening to Cody and Russ was like being present at an exchange between her own brothers. A strong sense of family was an integral part of who she was. She loved their frequent get-togethers and had missed Taylor dreadfully over the past year.

"Is it always like this between these two?" Christy asked her sister.

"Sometimes worse," Taylor answered.

"Russ was the ultimate traitor," Cody said, setting his coffee mug aside. "He married a dark-haired, blue-eyed woman, and worse, I wasn't even invited to the wedding."

"No one was," Mandy inserted as she came in from the kitchen, drying her hands on her apron skirt. "Not even me. Russ's very own sister."

"I swear you're never going to forgive me for that, are you?" Russ grumbled. "Just wait till you fall in love, little sister, then you might be more understanding."

Mandy straightened her spine and threw back her shoulders. Her eyes narrowed as she glared across the room at her brother. She reminded Christy so much of her older sister confronting their father that she nearly laughed out loud.

"It may come as a shock to you, big brother, but I've been in love several times." Mandy evidently considered herself a woman of the world.

Russ didn't hide his opinions on *that* issue. He rolled his eyes.

"Russ," Taylor said softly.

"Now what did I do?" he asked. At the rate he was going, his foot would remain permanently in his mouth. "All right, all right, I — *we* made a mistake by not including you in the wedding ceremony. There. Are you satisfied?"

"No. I want you to admit that I'm old

enough to be in love."

"Mandy!"

"Admit it." It was clear that brother and sister were often at odds, yet Christy sensed the deep and abiding love they shared.

"Don't look at me, Russ Palmer," Taylor said bluntly. "You got yourself into this."

"I suppose that at fifteen a mature teenage girl may have experienced her first taste of love."

"May have?" Mandy repeated. "That's not good enough."

"Hey, the girl wants blood," Cody murmured.

"She's likely to get it, too," Taylor said, apparently for Christy's benefit.

"All right, I'll admit it. There! *Now* are you satisfied?"

Mandy smiled graciously and nodded. "Thank you, brother dearest."

"You're welcome, sister sweetest." He turned his attention away from Mandy. "Listen," Russ said, looking at Cody and Christy and then back at his friend. "If you two ever get married, whether it's to each other or anyone else, take my advice and don't elope."

"If Mandy was upset about not being at the wedding, that was nothing compared to how strongly Mom and Dad felt about it,"

Taylor said. "Dad seemed to feel I'd cheated him out of an important part of fatherhood by not letting him escort me down the aisle."

From somewhere deep inside, Christy forced a smile. This talk about weddings was making her decidedly uncomfortable. What her sister said was true enough; her parents had been bitterly disappointed not to hold a large wedding for their oldest daughter. It was one of the reasons they were so pleased when Christy announced that she and James would be getting married. Almost immediately they'd started talking about the church ceremony, with a reception and dance to follow.

"I think it's time for us to go, don't you?" Cody said to Christy, unfolding his long legs and standing. He walked across the room in three strides. "See you later, Taylor, Eric. Oh, and you, too." He nodded at Russ with a grin. "Thanks for dinner, everyone."

"Where are you two headed?" Russ wanted to know, making no effort to disguise his interest.

"Out." Cody turned to Christy, and his smile was like the warm fingers of sunlight in winter. They'd known each other such a short while, and it seemed inconceivable that she could feel like this. But she did.

The feelings she and Cody shared were too complex to put into words.

"When will you be back?" Russ asked his sister-in-law, as if he wasn't completely convinced his best friend was safe in her company.

"Who appointed you my guardian angel?" Cody asked sarcastically, his eyebrows raised.

"I'm only looking out for your best interests," Russ explained, continuing the game. "Good grief, man, she's pretty with dark hair and blue eyes. We learned way back in the sixth grade that those are the ones to watch out for. You've got to be careful. Look what happened to me!"

"What did happen to you?" Taylor asked, her brow wrinkling with the question.

"You should know. Before I realized it, I was saddled with a wife. I don't mind telling you, Franklin, I'm worried about you."

"If I'm responsible for the security of an entire county, you can trust me to take care of myself."

"Saddled?" Taylor asked, her voice ominously low. "You found yourself *saddled* with a wife?"

Russ instantly looked guilty. "Maybe saddled wasn't the best word."

"Then I suggest you search for another."

"Ah . . ." Russ rubbed his hand across his neck.

"He's talking off the top of his head," Cody said, defending his friend. He turned toward Russ. "If I were you, I'd plead for leniency and remind her how crazy in love you are."

"How about I was *favored* with a wife?" Russ muttered. He seemed quite pleased with his choice of word.

Taylor glanced at Christy, a smile playing at the corners of her mouth, then shook her head. "You'll have to do better than that."

"Taylor, come on, I'm having a serious discussion with my friend here. All I'm trying to do is impart a few words of wisdom before Cody makes the same . . . before he ends up . . ."

"Ends up what?" Taylor prompted.

It took Russ a moment to answer. "Blessed?" he offered, confident he'd smoothed things over.

"Blessed is an acceptable word."

"I think we should get out of here while the getting's good, don't you?" Cody asked, reaching for Christy's hand, entwining their fingers.

"I couldn't agree with you more." The solid ground beneath her feet seemed to shift as she realized that once they were alone she'd need to explain about James. Dragging in a steadying breath, she looked at Taylor. "I won't be gone long."

"If I get worried, I'll call the sheriff," Taylor teased.

The phone rang, and Mandy shot out of the living room.

Russ escorted Christy and Cody to the back door.

Mandy appeared, stretching the long telephone cord into the kitchen. She seemed confused as she held out the receiver to Russ. "I think it must be a wrong number. Maybe you should talk to him."

"All right."

Cody chuckled. "I never thought I'd be grateful for a phone call. I had the impression Russ was going to make us listen to more of his pearls of wisdom."

They were all the way down the steps when the back door swung open with enough force to send it crashing shut.

"Christy." Russ stood on the top of the steps, hands on his hips, his eyes squinting against the setting sun.

"Yes?" She turned to face her brother-in-law. The humor in his eyes had been replaced with a fierce anger that transformed his handsome features.

Cody took a step forward. "What is it?"

"The phone," Russ said. "It's for Christy. Someone named James Wilkens."

She gasped softly before she could stop herself.

"He claims he's her fiancé."

FIVE

"Cody, please," Christy began, her heart in her eyes. "I can explain."

"You mean it's true?" Russ shouted.

"It's not as bad as it sounds — if you'd take the time to listen." Both of her hands gripped Cody's forearm as she boldly held on to him, not wanting to let him go for fear she'd never see him again.

"Are you engaged or not?" Cody asked. His dark eyes burned into hers, searing her conscience far more deeply than any words he could've spoken.

"I was going to tell you about James. . . ."

Cody's face tensed as though she'd delivered a crippling blow to his abdomen. He lowered his gaze to her hands, which clenched his arm tightly.

"I see." The two words were cold, his voice remote.

She moistened her lips, unsure she could trust her voice. "Please let me explain."

"What's there to say? It's simple, isn't it? Either you're engaged or you're not." He pulled himself free and turned his back to her.

"Cody." She tried once more, hating the way her voice wobbled as she pleaded for patience and understanding.

One stern look told her he wasn't willing to grant her either. Her heart seized painfully as she slowly dropped her hands and stepped away from him.

Without another word, Cody climbed inside his Cherokee, slammed the door and drove away as if the very demons of hell were in hot pursuit.

Christy went completely still. She couldn't move. Couldn't breathe.

How long she stood there, Christy had no idea. Nor could she put order to her thoughts. Just a few minutes ago she'd been sitting across the room from Cody, laughing with him, sharing secret smiles, her whole being permeated with gladness and joy. How natural it had seemed to be together. As natural as the sun setting. As natural as rain.

"Are you going to talk to your fiancé or not?" Russ demanded, his voice sharp with censure.

Christy stared at him for a moment before

she realized James was still on the phone. Nevertheless, she stood where she was and watched the plume of dust that trailed behind Cody's vehicle. After a while it faded away, taking with it the promise of something wonderful.

Russ waited for her at the top of the porch steps. Christy lowered her eyes as she moved past him. He didn't need to say anything for her to feel his reprimand.

The telephone receiver was resting on a small table in the hallway. Christy dragged in a deep, calming breath and reached for it. "Hello, James." She prayed her voice revealed none of her turmoil.

"Christy. How are you?" He sounded anxious, concerned.

"Fine, just fine. Taylor had the baby, but I suppose you've heard about that already. I doubt Mom and Dad could keep quiet about Eric. He really is precious." She knew she was chattering but couldn't seem to make herself stop. "Montana is a beautiful state. I haven't seen much of Cougar Point yet, except the bowling alley. I had breakfast there the other morning, only it was really the middle of the afternoon — the day Eric was born, actually."

"You ate breakfast at a bowling alley?"

"There's a restaurant there and the food's

good — excellent, in fact."

"That's nice."

"How are you?" Christy felt obliged to ask.

"Fine. I miss you." He dropped his voice slightly as if he'd admitted something he shouldn't. "The office seems empty with you away."

James wasn't a man who was comfortable with expressing his emotions. Showing affection was difficult for him. The fact that he'd called and said he missed her was practically equivalent to another man standing on a rooftop and shouting at the top of his voice that he was madly in love.

"I . . . I've been busy."

"I was hoping you'd call me."

His disappointment echoed in each word.

"I'm sorry, James, really I am. It's just that everything happened so fast. I didn't even have a chance to unpack my bags before Taylor went into labor. She came home from the hospital today, and we . . . we were just having dinner." That was a slight exaggeration, but she needed an excuse to get off the phone before she did something stupid like weep uncontrollably or tell him about Cody.

"You're having dinner? Why didn't you say something sooner? No wonder it took you so long to get to the phone."

Christy leaned against the wall, closed her eyes and swallowed. She felt guilty about by her minor deception, contaminated by the way she was deceiving him in an effort to cut short this painful conversation.

James deserved so much more than this. The guilt was killing her, and it demanded all the self-control she possessed to keep from blurting everything out.

"I'll let you go, but before I do I want you to know I got the diamond back from the jeweler. It'll be ready when you return from your sister's."

"Oh, g-great," she stammered, trying to inject some enthusiasm into her voice.

"Goodbye, Christy. Give my regards to Taylor and her husband and congratulate them both for me."

"I will. Bye, James. Don't work too hard."

"No, I won't."

She replaced the receiver, her fingers curled tensely around it as she waited for the recriminations to rain down on her. She felt an overwhelming sense of wrongdoing, a surge of remorse.

Raised voices came at her from inside the living room.

"The least you can do is listen to her," Christy heard Taylor shout.

"What possible explanation could she

have? Either she's engaged or she isn't."

"Listen to me, Russ Palmer. I won't have you yelling at my sister. Whatever's happening between her and Cody is her business. It doesn't have anything to do with us."

"Like hell I'm going to stay out of it. We're talking about Cody here — my best friend. I thought he was your friend, too."

"He is."

"Then you can't expect to sit idly by and watch him get hurt."

"Please," Christy said, stepping into the room. She couldn't bear to have them arguing over her. "Please . . . don't fight."

The room went silent, a silence so intense it seemed to throb like a giant heart. Taylor's gaze, clouded with doubt and uncertainty, locked with Christy's. Russ's eyes were filled with reproach.

Russ and Taylor continued to stare at her. Russ was angry and made no effort to disguise his feelings. Taylor, usually so strong and confident, couldn't hide her confusion.

Christy suspected her sister was as troubled as her husband. Only Taylor wouldn't allow herself to voice her misgivings because of family loyalty.

"Sit down," Taylor suggested. She motioned toward the recliner where Christy had sat earlier. "You're so pale. Are you sure you're all right?"

"Why didn't you tell us you were engaged?" Russ asked, barely giving her time to compose herself. "And if you and James are getting married, why aren't you wearing a ring?"

"Russ, please," Taylor said, "let her answer one question before hitting her with another." Directing her attention to Christy, Taylor widened her eyes. "We're waiting."

Folding her hands in her lap, Christy squeezed her fingers so tightly they hurt. "James asked me to marry him two days before I left Seattle."

"He didn't give you an engagement ring?"

"Of course . . . it's being sized now."

"I see," Taylor said, frowning. "And you didn't mention it to anyone? Do Mom and Dad know? I'm your sister, for heaven's sake! The least you could've done was mention it to me."

"Taylor," Russ said gruffly, then reminded her of her own words. "She can only answer one question at a time."

"I didn't have a chance to tell you when I first arrived. Remember? Then first thing the next morning you went into labor and . . . I met Cody."

"You had no business leading him on,"

Russ snapped.

"I didn't mean to," she cried, and raked her fingers though her short hair, praying Taylor and Russ wouldn't condemn her. "It just . . . happened. We were both so excited about the baby and afterward we went out to eat. Then Cody drove me home and . . . and I knew he was going to kiss me. I realize it was a mistake not to say anything to him, but I was afraid . . ." Afraid that if she *had* said something he wouldn't have touched her, and she'd wanted his kiss so much.

Unable to meet her sister's eyes, she glanced at the coffee table as the tears spilled down her cheeks.

"Who's this James character, anyway?" Russ asked Taylor. "Did we meet him?"

She nodded. "He's the attorney Christy introduced to us last summer."

"Not the . . ." He hesitated.

"Why didn't you tell me?" Taylor apparently considered it a personal affront that Christy had kept the news to herself. "We had plenty of time to talk while I was in the hospital and you were there every day."

"I tried," Christy said in her own defense. "But every time I mentioned James, you changed the subject. And when I finally managed to drag him back into the conversation, you started telling me how dry and boring you think he is and what a mismatched couple we are. What was I supposed to do? Tell you I'd agreed to marry the man you'd just finished criticizing?"

"Oh, dear," Taylor whispered. "Now that you mention it, I do remember you trying to bring James into the conversation."

"Fine. You two got that settled, but what about Cody?" Russ stalked to the other side of the room and stared out the front window. "I can't, I *won't* let this happen to him a second time. Not when it's in my power to prevent it." Gradually he turned around, his shoulders squared and his jaw tightly clenched.

"A second time?" Christy echoed.

When Russ didn't respond right away, she looked at her sister, who was busy with Eric. Either that or she was avoiding eye contact. "Taylor?"

"It happened several years ago," Russ began grudgingly. "A woman by the name of Rebecca Morgan moved into town. She was from somewhere in the south and had the sweetest manners you can imagine. She was the type of woman a man could fall in love with. Becca was perfect. Beautiful. Demure. Charming and . . ." Russ shook his head. "Who would've guessed?"

"Guessed what?" Christy asked.

"Becca made it obvious from the moment she moved into town that she was attracted to Cody. Every time he turned around there she was, batting her eyes at him, doing those things you women do to let a man know you're interested."

"I could make a comment here, but I won't," Taylor muttered.

"Soon Becca and Cody were seeing a lot of each other. You have to understand, Cody isn't easily taken in, especially by a pretty woman. Until recently." He frowned at Christy as he said it. "But Becca did more than interest him. For the first time in his life, Cody was in love. It showed in everything he said and did.

"Cody's always been popular with the folks around here, and his happiness seemed to rub off on everyone. Most folks liked Becca, too. They couldn't help it. There was plenty of talk about the two of them getting married." Russ walked over to the ottoman and sat down. "A month or so after she moved into town, a series of baffling robberies started happening."

"You don't mean to say Becca . . ."

"Not her personally. She was part of a team. They worked a scam in small cities all across the western states. Apparently the heat was on in several of the larger cities, and she and her partner decided to try their hand in smaller towns. They were successful, too. Becca would move someplace and get involved with a deputy from the local sheriff's office. One way or another she'd get information about shipments of money to the town banks. Then she'd pass that information to her partner. It was all cleverly done. Whenever a shipment of cash was due to arrive, Becca would make sure she was nowhere nearby. Two banks were robbed, and a couple of stores lost valuable equipment all within the second month she was in town. But no one suspected her. How could they? She was just as sweet as honey."

"How long did it take Cody to realize it was Becca?"

"Not long, a few weeks, but he felt like the biggest fool who ever lived and you'll never convince him differently. He took responsibility for everything, blamed himself for not picking up on the scam sooner."

"But he loved her. Trusted her."

Russ's dark gaze collided with Christy's. "I know. He arrested her and her partner and testified against them."

"Surely no one blamed Cody!"

"No, everyone in town was as taken in by her as he was. But Cody felt as responsible as if he'd personally handed over the money. It's his job to protect and to serve and he felt he'd let the entire county down, although he worked his fool head off until every penny was returned. Even that wasn't enough. Cody felt he had to resign from the department."

"No." Christy's response was immediate. True, she'd only known Cody a short while, but in that time she'd learned how important law enforcement was to him.

"Thankfully some of us were able to talk some sense into him. He made the mistake of falling in love with the wrong woman — but then again, it was all due to his efforts that Becca and her friend were caught. If it hadn't been for Cody, no one knows how long their little scam would've worked or how many other communities would've been bilked. Unfortunately Cody didn't see it that way."

"He's only human." Christy felt a burning need to defend him.

"Becca used him. But worse than that, she made him feel like an idiot. It's taken three years for him to live it down, at least in his own mind. The way most folks figure it, Cody did Montana a good deed by putting Becca Morgan and her partner behind bars."

"That's why he wouldn't run for sheriff until last year?" Taylor asked, shifting the baby in her arms.

"It's been his life's dream to be elected sheriff of Custer County, but it took all this time for him to agree to run. I suppose he felt he had to prove his worth all over again. The crazy part is that he could've won hands down *any* year, including the year he was involved with Becca."

"I didn't know," Taylor said softly.

"It's not something that's talked about a lot," Russ explained. "The subject is such a painful one, it's best forgotten."

"Then Becca's still in prison?" Christy managed to ask. Learning how Cody had been deceived was painful for her, too. The knowledge that justice had been done somehow made it easier to accept.

"From what I understand, she's tried to contact Cody a few times, claiming she really was in love with him, and still is. To hear her tell it, she was a helpless pawn in all this. She says she was a victim of blackmail. But Cody won't have anything to do with her."

"I can certainly understand that," Taylor said.

"You aren't comparing me to Becca, are you?" Christy asked bluntly, feeling even more wretched.

"You're no thief," Russ said abruptly. "I'm not worried about you bilking the good citizens of Cougar Point, if that's what you think. No . . ." He rubbed the back of his neck. "After Becca something changed in Cody. He rarely dated. He closed himself off, became more pensive, introspective. It was as if he'd lost trust in women."

Taylor nodded. "I can't say I really blame him."

"I don't, either," Christy added, realizing as she did so that she was condemning herself.

Russ frowned. "That's why I was so pleased about what happened after he met you. When he looked at you, it was like seeing the old Cody all over again, the man who smiled and joked and didn't take everything so seriously. I don't know what went on between you." He hesitated and glanced at his wife. "Taylor's right when she says it isn't any of my business, but I won't stand by and let you take advantage of him."

"I wouldn't . . . I couldn't."

"Then why didn't you tell him you were engaged?"

Christy felt as if she'd been backed into a corner. "I planned to. I never intended to keep it a secret, but I needed time to think.

You may not believe this, but I'd hoped to talk to Cody about James tonight. I was going to tell him everything."

"Are you planning on marrying James?" Taylor asked, her eyes seeking Christy's.

The question came as a shock. "No. I couldn't — not after meeting Cody."

"Then why didn't you break the engagement when you had the chance?" Russ asked. "You were just talking to him. It would've been a simple matter to tell him then."

"I can't do it over the phone," Christy said, jerking her head upward. "James is a good man. He deserves better than that. He hasn't done anything wrong. I hate to hurt him. . . ." She paused when hot tears threatened to spill down her face. Biting her lower lip, she drew in a shuddering breath.

"Christy's right." Taylor's words cut through the emotion of the moment. "This is a delicate situation. You can't expect her to call James and break off the engagement. That would be heartless. This is best done in person. James may be a bit dull, but he's a decent human being."

"Is . . . is there any chance Cody will talk to me?" Christy wanted to drive into town and explain that she had no intention of going through with the marriage.

"I doubt he'll have anything to do with you," Russ answered, confirming her worst fears.

"Wait until tomorrow," Taylor advised. "Give him an opportunity to think everything through."

"He asked me out to dinner. . . . But I'm not sure if he'll show up."

"He won't," Russ said. "I know him better than anyone, and I can tell you, as far as he's concerned, whatever was between you is over."

Christy's shoulders sagged with defeat. "I was afraid of that."

"Don't make it sound so hopeless," Taylor muttered.

"She's engaged, for crying out loud. What do you expect Cody to do?" Russ said. "Ignore it? He isn't going to do that."

"But I have every intention of breaking off the engagement."

"I doubt that'll make any difference to him. I'll be surprised if he even listens to you."

"That's not true," Taylor said confidently. "Cody's a reasonable man, and it's obvious that he's attracted to you."

"He isn't anymore." Russ shook his head for emphasis.

Taylor shot daggers at her husband. "Russ

Palmer, kindly allow me to finish."

"Feel free, but you've got to understand. After Becca, Cody doesn't have a lot of trust in the opposite sex."

"My sister isn't another Becca," Taylor insisted.

"You and I know that."

A short silence followed before Christy said, "Cody's smart enough to know it, too." She wanted to believe that. Needed to believe it. But whether that was the case or not was something she'd soon discover.

Cody slammed his fist against the steering column. He was parked on the ridge that overlooked Cougar Point and had been sitting there for the past hour, collecting his thoughts.

Frustration and anger mounted with each passing minute. Drawing in a deep breath, he rubbed his face with both hands, certain he'd almost made a world-class fool of himself for the second time.

When was he going to learn? Women weren't to be trusted. Especially pretty blue-eyed ones who looked as pure as freshly fallen snow. On the outside they were all sweetness, but inside . . . His thoughts skidded to an abrupt halt despite his best efforts to think badly of Christy.

113

He couldn't compare Becca with Taylor's sister. The two women had little, if anything, in common. Becca was a con artist. Christy wouldn't know how to deceive anyone.

But she had.

She'd deceived him.

Once more he rubbed his hand down his face. Had she really? Hadn't she said there was something she needed to tell him? He'd stood in Russ's kitchen, looked into her beautiful eyes and had seen for himself the turmoil inside her. He'd been unable to grasp what was troubling her.

But right now all Cody could think about was himself. For the first time in years he'd been able to feel again. For the first time in years he'd been whole.

The only thing he felt now was an ache that cut far deeper than anything he'd known before. His feelings for Christy had been a cruel joke.

"You don't honestly expect Cody's going to come, do you?" Taylor asked as Christy sprayed her carefully styled hair. She'd spent the past half hour fussing with her makeup and hair, hoping that if she looked her best, it would lend her confidence.

"No. But I want to be ready in case he does."

"You've been restless all day," her sister said.

"I know. I can't help it. Oh, Taylor, I can't bear to let things end this way between Cody and me. Everything felt so . . . so right with us."

"It's hard, isn't it?"

She nodded, fighting the need to rush to him and make him understand. "His eyes were so cold. I didn't know anyone could look so . . ." She couldn't think of a word strong enough to describe her fears.

For much of the night she'd wrestled with the sheets and blankets, trying to find a comfortable position. Once she did and closed her eyes, the disdainful look on Cody's face would pop into her mind. Her eyes would fly open, and the need to explain to him would dominate her thoughts again.

She'd spent most of the night composing what she was going to say. All day she'd been mentally rehearsing it so when the time came she'd be ready.

But she didn't feel ready now. She felt uneasy and scared, as if nothing she could say or do would make a difference.

"If he doesn't come, what do you plan to do?"

"Go to him," Christy said firmly. "He made a date, and he's going to keep it whether he wants to or not."

A quick smile flashed from Taylor's eyes, and her lips quivered with the effort to suppress it. "I see."

"I mean it. If Cody isn't man enough to give me a chance to explain, then he deserves what he's going to get."

"And what's that?"

"I haven't decided yet, but I'll think of something."

"Yes, I'm sure you will," Taylor said on her way out of the bathroom.

Once she was finished, Christy joined her sister, who was busy with dinner preparations. "Let me help," she insisted, feeling guilty that Taylor was stuck with the cooking. The very reason Christy was in Montana was to help with the household chores while Taylor recuperated.

"Don't be silly. I'm perfectly fine. Besides, you might mess up your makeup." Leaning against the counter, Taylor surveyed Christy's attire. "Personally I'm betting Cody's not going to be able to take his eyes off you."

"Oh, Taylor, do you really think so?" Looking her best was important to Christy. If Cody was going to slam the door in her face, which was a distinct possibility, then

116

she wanted him to know what he was missing.

"There's something different about you," Taylor went on to say, her expression somber. She crossed her arms and cocked her head to one side.

"You mean the eyeliner. I'm using a different shade."

"No, this doesn't have anything to do with eyeliner. You're not the same Christy I left when I moved away from Seattle."

"I'm older," Christy said, "and hopefully more mature."

Taylor paused to consider that. "I suppose that's part of it, but there's more."

"Oh?"

"You were always the 'good daughter.' "

"You make it sound like you were the bad one, and that isn't the least bit true."

"But we both know I love an argument," Taylor said, "and Dad was always willing to comply. We were so often at odds."

"But you and Dad loved and respected each other. It wasn't like some families."

"I know. It's just that we're so different. About the worst thing I can remember you doing was running around the house with a pair of scissors in your hand."

"I did go swimming in the community pool without a bathing cap that one time, remember?"

"Ah, yes, I'd forgotten about that. You renegade!"

They laughed. Taylor was right; Christy had never caused a problem, never been in trouble. The good daughter. Too good, in some ways.

"You realize Mom and Dad are going to be disappointed when they find out you aren't going to marry James."

"Probably more disappointed than James," Christy joked.

Taylor frowned slightly. "Are you sure you're doing the right thing?"

The question was unexpected. "Of course. Very soon after I met Cody, I knew I should never have agreed to marry James. I . . ."

"Then why did you?"

"Well . . . because we're friends and we'd been working together a lot, and it just seemed . . . like a good idea."

"Your decision had nothing to do with Mom and Dad?"

"I . . . ah . . ."

"I don't mean to pressure you or sound like a know-it-all, but if you check your motives, I think you might discover that you accepted James's proposal for all the wrong reasons. It suited Mom and Dad for you to marry him, and you went along with it because you were trying to please them. Am I right?"

"I . . ." Christy lowered her eyes as a tingling extended from her stomach to her arms and down her fingers. She loved her parents so much and wanted to make them proud of her. Her marrying James would certainly have done that. Christy had been so concerned about doing what her parents thought was right that she'd never considered if it was best for her.

"Christy?"

"You make me sound so weak, so insecure."

"You're not. You're loving and gentle and good. James is a fine young man, but he's not the one for you."

Without question her parents would be upset with her, but in time they'd realize she was doing what was best for both her and James.

Christy left the Lazy P soon afterward, not waiting to see if Cody was going to come for her or not. From the way he'd left the evening before, she suspected he had no intention of keeping their dinner date.

She found his place without a problem and parked her car. She took several minutes to compose herself before making her way to the front door.

An eternity passed before he answered her knock. "Christy?"

"I believe we have a dinner date," she said boldly, damning her voice for shaking. She didn't want him to guess how terribly nervous this confrontation made her.

"A dinner date? You and me? Forget it, sweetheart. If you want to go out, call your fiancé."

Six

"I'm not going to marry James," Christy explained in a voice that demanded Cody listen to her and at the same time begged for his understanding. Cody wasn't in the mood to do either. From the moment he'd left Christy the night before, he'd fought to push every thought of her from his mind.

With very little success.

"Who you marry or don't marry is none of my business," he said, his words sharp and abrupt.

Christy flinched at his disdain, and it was all Cody could do to keep from reaching for her and asking her forgiveness.

"Please, if you'd give me a chance to explain. . . ."

She was so beautiful, with her cobalt-blue eyes and sweet, innocent face. Until he'd met Christy and Taylor, Cody had never seen eyes that precise shade of blue.

He groaned inwardly, struggling against

the need to take her in his arms and bask in her softness. Equally strong was the instinctive urge to protect his heart and his orderly life from the havoc she was sure to bring.

Cody was the sheriff-elect, but there was little that could terrify him the way this woman did. It was essential to keep his eyes off her. Everything about her was sensual and provocative. It was difficult enough to fight her, but the battle grew even fiercer as he struggled with his own desires. This was much harder than he'd ever imagined it would be.

"At least talk to me."

Her voice was soft and compelling. The mere sound could drive him straight through the bounds of what was fast becoming his limited self-control.

"I think you should leave."

There, he'd said it. He didn't mean it, but he'd said it, and that little bit of resistance lent him a sense of control, which had been sadly lacking to this point. Christy wasn't aware of that, but he was.

"I'm not leaving until you've listened to me."

"Then you're going to have to do your talking from the street." It astonished him how forcefully he came across. He blocked the doorway as he leaned indolently against the jamb, trying his best to suggest that he hadn't a care in the world.

She hesitated, then surprised him by nodding. "Fine. If that's what it takes, I'll shout at you from the middle of the street, loud enough for the entire block to hear."

"You're wasting your time." He'd played these games with another woman once, and he wasn't about to fall into that trap a second time.

Feeling suddenly confident, he straightened, leaned forward and braced his hands against her shoulders, keeping her at arm's length. It was a risk to touch her, but one he was prepared to take. Perhaps he felt the need to convince himself that he could be close to her and not want to kiss her. . . .

His plan backfired the instant she looked directly up at him. To complicate matters, she flattened her hands on his chest. His heart reacted immediately, and he was sure she could feel the effect she had on him. Maybe touching her wasn't such a smart move, after all.

"I meant what I said." He narrowed his eyes, hoping she'd take the hint and leave. In the same breath he prayed she wouldn't.

"You have every right to be angry," Christy continued, her eyes pleading with him. "I don't blame you. I intended to tell you about James and me. Remember when we were in the kitchen before dinner? I told you there was something I had to talk to you about."

She didn't give him a chance to answer. Not that it mattered; he did remember, all too well.

"It was never my intention to mislead you. I would've explained everything except James phoned before I had the chance."

Cody felt himself weakening. This wasn't supposed to be happening. He should be a tower of strength. A bastion of fortitude. With little more than a shrug of his shoulders he ought to send her packing. One woman had mercilessly used him before. Only an idiot would allow it to happen again.

"I realized the first time you kissed me that I could never marry James," she persisted. "Maybe even before then. I know it should've been a simple decision, but it wasn't. I had to think everything through. The answer was so obvious, so clear — but it frightened me."

She was frightened! Cody was shaking in his boots!

He dropped his hands; touching her had been a tactical error.

"So you've broken it off?" he asked, hating the way his hopes rose at the possibility that she was free.

Christy dropped her eyes. "Not exactly. But I promise you I will the minute I get back to Seattle."

Cody's blood turned to ice. So she intended to string him along. At least she was honest about it, but frankly that didn't count for much.

"I know it sounds bad," she said softly. "You might think it'd be better if I told James now. I thought so myself, but then I realized it wouldn't be right. James doesn't deserve to be treated so heartlessly. He's a good man — it would be wrong to call him and just tell him I'd met someone else. It's cruel to do it over the phone."

Cody snorted a soft laugh. She was a candidate for the loony bin if she expected him to buy into that. Either she was engaged to James or she wasn't. Either the wedding was on or it was off. As simple as that.

"All right," she said, and he could see her fighting to hold on to her composure. "If you can't accept that, I'll phone James and talk to him right now."

"Fine." He led her into the house and didn't stop until he reached the kitchen phone. Feeling slightly cocky, he lifted the receiver and handed it to her, fully expecting her not to go through with the call. She was putting on a brave front, but he was sure she had no intention of following through.

She stared at the receiver for a moment before taking it out of his hand. When she did, Cody saw how deathly pale she'd gone.

She offered him a quick, reassuring smile. "You're right," she said weakly. "I shouldn't be thinking about James's feelings at a time like this. You have feelings, too. It's probably best to get this over with now. James will understand. I know he will." As if her fingers weighed a thousand pounds, she lifted her hand and slowly punched out a series of numbers, then closed her eyes as she waited. "He's probably still at the office."

After what seemed like an inordinate amount of time, and a short conversation with the receptionist, Christy replaced the receiver. "James already left. He must be home by now. I'll try there — only . . ." She looked up at him, her eyes wide and full of tension. She was willing to do this because Cody demanded it of her, but it was so hard. To know she was humiliating *James,* causing him pain . . .

"Only what?" he prompted.

"Could you kiss me? I seem to need it

right now."

His mouth found hers even before she'd finished speaking. He'd planned to brush his lips gently across hers. This wasn't the time for anything more.

To be on the safe side, he kissed her again — just so he'd know for a fact that he could walk away from her in the blink of an eye.

That was Cody's second tactical error of the evening.

She tasted like heaven, sweet and warm. His mouth continued to move over hers until her lips parted. She sighed deeply and sagged against him. Then she buried her face in the curve of his neck. Her breathing was as hard and uneven as his own. His hands were splayed across her back, and he held on to her with what little strength he'd managed to reserve.

"Give me a moment and I'll phone James at his house," she whispered, her voice raspy.

Cody framed her face in his hands. "No," he whispered.

"No?"

"I'm not happy with the situation, but you're right. Breaking the engagement by phone would be insensitive. I can wait until you get back to Seattle and talk to him face-to-face."

She lowered her eyes in gratitude, her

thick lashes sweeping her cheek. "Thank you."

He nodded.

"Oh, Cody, please believe me, I'm going to end it. I'm being as completely honest as I can."

"I know."

"You do?"

He nodded. He wrapped his arms around her and rested his chin on her head. "I don't know where that leaves us," he said. "Or even where we go from here."

"I don't, either," Christy whispered, but he felt her sigh of contentment as she relaxed against him.

"You're as jumpy as a grasshopper," Russ teased three days later. "I swear you keep looking out that window as though you expect the Mounted Police to come riding over the hill."

"Not the Mounted Police, just one handsome sheriff."

"Ah, so you're seeing Cody again."

"I've seen him every night this week." Christy could feel herself blush as she said it, which was exactly the reaction her brother-in-law was looking for.

"Quit teasing my sister," Taylor said. She was sitting at the kitchen table, Eric nestled in her arms, nursing greedily.

Every time Christy watched her sister with the baby, she felt astonished at how easily Taylor had taken to motherhood. She acted as though she'd been around infants all her life. She seemed so comfortable, so *confident* with her son, whether she was breast feeding him or diapering or rocking him to sleep.

"Where's Cody taking you this afternoon?" Taylor asked, glancing up at her.

"He wouldn't say. It's supposed to be a surprise, but I have a sneaking suspicion we're headed into the wild blue yonder." At her sister's raised eyebrows, she explained. "I think he's planning to take me for a plane ride. He told me earlier that he has his private license and twice now he's mentioned flying."

"I thought you were afraid of planes," Taylor commented. When it was first decided that Christy would come to Montana, she'd immediately rejected the idea of flying into Miles City. Driving to Montana appealed to her far more. Neither Taylor nor their mother had pressed the issue.

"I'm not excited about flying," Christy admitted.

"But you don't mind going up in a plane with Cody?"

"No." She trusted him beyond question.

Enough to place her life in his hands.

"If I were you, I'd make sure his little surprise doesn't involve horses," Russ warned, and his eyes connected with his wife's as though they were sharing some well-kept secret.

"Cody doesn't ride that often."

Russ poured himself a cup of coffee and joined Taylor at the kitchen table. He smiled at his son while speaking to Christy. "You certainly seem to know a great deal about the sheriff's habits."

"I . . ." Christy could feel warmth invade her cheeks. She hated the way she blushed whenever the subject of Cody was introduced.

She and Cody had spent every available moment together. With her vacation vanishing like melting snow, each day was more precious than the one before. It was as if they were cramming several months of a relationship into two short weeks.

Cody wasn't pleased that she remained technically engaged to James, but he'd graciously accepted the situation. It wasn't easy for him, but he never questioned her about the other man, or brought James into their conversation.

For his part, Cody had never said anything to Christy about Becca and the way he'd been duped by the other woman. Knowing what she did made her more sensitive to his needs, made her love him all the more.

Christy did love Cody. This wasn't infatuation or hormones or anything else. For some reason, unknown to them both, they were meant to be together. She knew it. He knew it. Yet Christy never spoke of her feelings, and neither did Cody.

She understood his hesitancy. He couldn't talk freely about their relationship while James was still part of her life.

Once she was back in Seattle and had broken the engagement to James, then and only then would she tell Cody she loved him. And he in turn would be free to tell her what she already knew.

Christy would've liked to hear it sooner, but if Cody could display this much patience, she could do no less.

"I don't know when we'll be back," Christy said. "Is there anything I can do for you before I leave?" she asked, looking at Taylor.

Her sister grinned. "Just have a good time."

"I will." She was already having the time of her life.

"I was in town earlier today," Russ said.

He paused to be sure he had their full attention.

"So? You go into town at least twice a week," Taylor reminded him.

"Noah Williams, who works at the insurance agency, stopped me." Once more he hesitated as if this news was significant.

"Old Man Williams stops anybody who'll listen to him," Taylor interjected. "That man is the biggest gossip in three counties, and you know it."

Russ rubbed the side of his jaw. "Yeah, I suppose I do."

"Would you say what's on your mind and be done with it?" Taylor grumbled.

Russ chuckled. "All right. Noah claimed he'd heard that the sheriff's about to take a wife. A pretty one, too. He said word has it she's a relative of mine."

"Oh?" Christy asked, willingly playing into his hands. "And did this relative of yours have a name?"

Christy remembered Cody introducing her to the town's sole insurance agent. He'd also told her that Noah Williams was well acquainted with most folks' business, whether they were his clients or not.

"Said he didn't recall the name, but he thought it was something like Cathy or Christine. Or Christabel."

"Funny. Very funny," Christy muttered, looking out the window, hoping to see Cody's truck.

"I'm telling you right now," Russ said, chuckling again, "the secret's out. The sheriff's gonna take himself a wife."

The next afternoon, Christy was lying on her back in a meadow not far from the ranch house, chewing on a long blade of grass. Cody had taken her flying the previous day, just as she'd guessed, and the experience had been exhilarating, not frightening at all. He lay beside her now, staring at the darkening sky. A series of clouds was rolling in, obliterating the sun, but they'd both decided to ignore the threat of rain.

"Looks like there's a storm coming," Cody said.

"Let it. I don't mind, do you?"

"That depends." He rolled onto his stomach and leaned on his elbows as he gazed lovingly down at her. He didn't seem any more eager to leave the site of their picnic than Christy.

The afternoon had been ideal. Cody had arrived at the house early in the day, and Christy had met him with a basket full of goodies. Russ complained that she was taking enough food to feed a small army . . . of ants.

"Depends on what?" she asked, smiling up at him.

"On who I'm with." As if he couldn't stop himself, he leaned over her and pressed his mouth to hers. Then his lips moved along the side of her face and into her hair. He paused and went still as he breathed in the scent of the cologne she'd dabbed behind her ears.

Other than the few kisses they'd exchanged over the past days, Cody hadn't touched her. It wasn't that he didn't desire her, didn't need her. But he held himself back — held himself in check.

Christy understood and in many ways approved.

The physical attraction between them was more powerful than either had ever experienced. It wasn't something to be trifled with.

He kissed her again lightly, softly, gently.

Christy slid her hands up his chest and put her arms around his neck. He kissed her again, his breath hot and quick. "We should stop now," he warned but made no effort to move away from her.

"Yes, I know," she concurred.

He brushed his thumb back and forth over

her moist lips as if gathering the needed resolve to pull away from her. She gazed up into his dark, troubled eyes and saw his hesitation. His hands were trembling as he started to roll away from her.

"No." Her cry was instinctive. Urgent.

"Christy . . ."

"Shh." She sank her fingers into his hair at the sides of his lean, rugged face, raised her head from the soft patch of grass and touched her mouth to his.

His hands tangled with her short curls as he moved the upper half of his body over hers, anchoring her to the ground. Their frenzied kissing seemed to go on and on.

"Enough," he said breathlessly. "We have to stop."

Christy wanted him so desperately; the hunger to love him all but consumed her, and she moved fitfully beneath him.

"Christy," he said, "we're headed for trouble if we don't stop . . . *now.*"

"I thought sheriffs were trained to deal with any kind of trouble." Her tongue outlined his mouth even as she spoke.

Cody moaned.

Christy sighed.

There didn't seem to be anything strong enough in this world or the next to pull them apart. Christy felt as if she'd been created for this man, for this moment. The love between them was as inevitable as the setting sun. As natural as the ocean waves caressing the shore or the wind stirring the trees. Her blood seemed to vibrate in sympathy, a vibration that grew more insistent — until she realized something was amiss. It wasn't her blood that was pounding in her veins, but rain that was pounding the earth. The clouds burst over them, drenching Christy within seconds.

Cody brought his hands to her face, framing it as he slowly raised his head. His eyes sought hers.

"Cody, it's pouring!"

He responded by kissing her again. "You taste too sweet to move."

"You're getting soaked."

"So are you." He grinned. "And I don't mind if you don't."

"I don't."

"Good." Once more his mouth connected with hers. A moment later, Christy leaned against him. "We . . . almost made love."

"I promised myself we wouldn't," he whispered. "And this is a promise I mean to keep." His hands closed around her upper arms. "Understand?"

Christy nodded.

"I mean it, Christy."

"Yes, sir." She teased him with a salute.

Deftly he reversed their positions, smoothly rolling over and taking her with him so she was poised above him. She straddled his hips and arched her head back as the rain pummeled her face. Brushing away her hair, she smiled at the dark, angry sky.

"I suppose I should be grateful," Cody murmured.

"For the rain? Why?"

"You know why."

"Yes," she whispered, "but in some ways I wish . . ." She let the rest fade, because they were aware of what would have happened if Mother Nature hadn't intervened when she did.

SEVEN

"You're *sure* you want to babysit?" Taylor asked, as though she expected Christy to change her mind.

"You're going," Christy said, ushering her older sister to the kitchen where Russ was waiting impatiently. It was the first time Taylor had left Eric, and she was having second thoughts.

"This night is for you and Russ."

"I know but —"

"I have the phone number to the restaurant, the home nurse, the doctor and the hospital. If anything the least bit out of the ordinary occurs, I'll phone someone, so quit worrying."

"Eric's never had a bottle," Taylor protested.

"It's still Mama's milk. He's a smart baby. He'll adjust." After Taylor had spent a long — and hilarious — afternoon learning how to operate the breast pump, each ounce was more precious than gold.

"Christy, I'm not convinced this is such a good idea, after all."

"Don't be ridiculous. Eric will probably sleep the entire time you're away."

"Are you going to let me take you to dinner or not?" Russ's voice boomed from the kitchen. "I'd like to remind you the reservation is for six." After a hard day on the ranch, Russ got too hungry to wait much beyond that for the evening meal.

Cody was the one who'd come up with the idea of the two of them babysitting Eric while Russ and Taylor took an evening for themselves. It was Christy's last night in Cougar Point. First thing in the morning she'd start the long drive across three states. Although she'd been gone less than two weeks, it felt as if an entire lifetime had passed.

"Cody's here," Russ called out. "Just how long does it take you women to put on a little war paint, anyway?" His voice lowered, and Christy could hear him conversing with the sheriff. Her brother-in-law was saying that Taylor and Christy were the two most beautiful women in the county as it was. He contended that they didn't need makeup, and he was having a heck of a time understanding why they bothered with it.

"Hold your horses," Taylor cried, poking her head out the bathroom door and calling down the hallway into the kitchen. "I'll only be a minute."

"Famous last words if I ever heard 'em," Russ grumbled.

As it turned out, her brother-in-law was right. Taylor spent an extra five minutes fussing with her hair and adding a dash of perfume to her wrists. When she'd finished, she checked Eric, gave Christy and Cody a long list of instructions, then reluctantly left the house with her husband.

Cody brought his arm around Christy as they stood on the back porch, watching Russ hold open the car door for Taylor. Christy smiled when Russ stole a lengthy kiss.

"Well," Cody said after Russ had pulled out of the yard, "they're off."

"I don't think they'll win any races."

"No," he chuckled, "I doubt they will." He turned her into his arms and kissed her softly.

"Oh, honestly," Mandy said, scooting past them and down the porch steps. "You two are as bad as Russ and Taylor. If it was me doing these PDAs, you can bet I'd be in big trouble. It seems to me that people over twenty-one get away with a whole lot more than they should."

"PDAs?" Christy asked. "What's that?"

"Public Displays of Affection," Cody whispered close to her ear. As if the temptation were too strong to resist, he caught her lobe between his teeth.

"Cody," she cried, "behave yourself."

"Hey, where are you going?" Cody demanded when Mandy started toward the barn. "I thought you were planning to stick around and chaperone the two of us."

"I'm going to the movies."

"In the barn?"

"Don't be cute with me, Cody Franklin. Just because you've been elected sheriff doesn't mean you can control *my* life."

"You're not the one I want to get cute with."

"Obviously. I figured you two would appreciate a little privacy. Billy Joe's driving me over to Melissa's, and I'm going to the movies with her. She got her license last week."

"I heard rumors along those lines," Cody said with a grin.

"Just don't go sending Bud or any of the other deputies out to tail us." Mandy wagged an accusing finger in Cody's direction. "I know you'd do it, too. Melissa's still a little nervous, and the last thing she needs is a sheriff's car following her into town."

"You think I'd radio for someone to follow her?" Cody sounded aghast that Mandy would even hint at something so dastardly.

"You'd do it if you thought you could." But she was smiling as she spoke.

Billy Joe, Russ's ranch foreman, stepped out from the barn, freshly shaved. His hair was wet and combed down against the sides of his head. "You ready?"

"Yup," Mandy said, walking toward his battered red pickup.

Taylor had explained that the foreman was interested in Melissa's widowed mother and had been seeing her for the past few months. Apparently Mandy and Melissa were working together to stage an evening alone for the two adults.

Eric wailed loudly, and after bidding Mandy farewell, Christy hurried inside the house and into the master bedroom. Eric was lying in the bassinet waiting for someone to answer his summons.

"What's the matter, big boy?" she asked, reaching for him. His damp bottom answered that question. "So you wet your diaper, did you?" she chided playfully, giving him her finger, which he gripped fiercely.

"I'll change him," Cody said from behind her.

Christy arched her brows in feigned shock. "This I've got to see."

"I'll have you know I've changed more than one diaper in my lifetime."

"That may be true, but it seems to me you took great delight in teasing Russ when he offered to change Eric."

"I've had more practice than Russ, that's all." Cody took a fresh diaper from the pile of folded ones on the dresser. "Both of my sisters have children, and being the generous uncle I am, I've helped out now and then. It's not nearly as difficult as Russ seems to think."

"All right, since you're so sure of yourself, go ahead and I'll see to our dinner." Carefully she handed Cody the baby, then walked to the kitchen.

Taylor had set a frozen pepperoni pizza on the kitchen counter. The only place in Cougar Point that served pizza was the bowling alley; Taylor could go without a lot of luxuries, but she needed her pizza. Every time she was in Miles City, she bought three or four pepperoni pizzas from a nationwide chain, brought them home and promptly froze them.

"I hope you're in the mood for pizza," Christy called, setting the gauge on the oven to the right temperature.

"You mean Taylor's willing to share one of hers? Without us having to ask?"

"I didn't even have to bribe her."

"I may volunteer to babysit more often," Cody said as he entered the kitchen, holding Eric against his shoulder. His large hand was pressed against the infant's tiny back.

Christy paused when she saw them, and her heart beat so fast, it actually hurt. Cody looked so natural with a baby in his arms. As natural as any father. Turning away in an effort to disguise her emotions, she clasped the counter with both hands and waited for the aching tenderness to pass.

She was engaged to an attorney in Seattle, a good friend she'd known for several years, and not once had she pictured him as a father. The fact that they'd likely have children someday had barely crossed her mind.

Yet here she was with Cody and her nephew, and the sight of this big, rugged man holding this precious child was enough to bring tears to her eyes.

"Christy, could you give me . . ." He hesitated when she didn't immediately respond. "Christy?"

She swallowed the lump in her throat, smeared the tears across her cheek and turned, smiling as brightly as she could. She doubted she'd be able to fool Cody, but she intended to try.

"What's wrong?" His question was filled with concern.

"Nothing . . ."

"If that's the case, then why are you crying?"

She didn't know how she could explain it, not without sounding as though she required long-term therapy. She was crazy in love with one man, and engaged to another. In a few hours she'd be leaving Cody behind. There were no guarantees, no pledges, no promises between them.

Nothing.

There couldn't be anything while she was engaged to James.

James. Two weeks away from him and she had trouble remembering what he looked like. Inconsequential details occurred to her — that he drank his tea with milk and hadn't worn a pair of jeans since he was thirteen years old. He was endearing, hardworking and brilliant.

And he loved her. At least he thought he did, the same way she'd once assumed she loved him.

The phone rang, startling Eric, who let out a loud wail. Cody whispered reassurances while patting the baby's back.

"I'll get that," Christy said, grateful for the intrusion. "It's probably Taylor calling to check up on us." She hurried into the hallway, wanting to catch the phone before it rang again and frightened Eric a second time.

"Hello," she sang out cheerfully. "This is Palmer's Pizza Parlor. May I take your order?" Taylor would get a kick out of that.

Silence followed.

"It appears I've dialed the wrong number," a male voice said stiffly.

"James? Oh, dear . . . I thought it was Taylor. This is Christy."

Cody heard Christy's laughter end two seconds after she answered the phone. He knew almost immediately that the man on the other end of the line was her fiancé.

Cody was instantly overwhelmed by confusion and an equally large dose of good old-fashioned jealousy. He was so resentful of Christy's engagement that a long painful moment passed before he could clear his head. He'd never been the jealous type, and now he was all but blinded by it.

He shouldn't have been surprised that James — he had trouble thinking about the other man without tightening his jaw — would call Christy. If Cody was the one engaged to her and she was a thousand miles away, he'd phone her, too. Frequently.

That realization, however, was no comfort. Before many more hours passed, Christy would be leaving Cougar Point. In another two days she'd be back with James. Her weeks with him in Montana would be little more than a fading memory.

Cody wasn't willing to kid himself any longer. There was no use trying to hide from it, or deny it or ignore it. He was in love with Christy Manning. He'd pledged a thousand times that he'd never allow this foolish emotion to take hold of his life again. So much for all the promises he'd made himself. So much for protecting his heart.

Dammit all, he was in love!

But Cody was realistic enough to put their relationship in the proper perspective. Or at least try. Christy was engaged to a hotshot Seattle attorney. He, on the other hand, was a backwoods sheriff. Christy might be infatuated with him now, but once she returned to the big city that could easily change. Believing these few days together meant more to her could be dangerous.

She was going to break the engagement. Or so she claimed. But now something was troubling her. Cody had sensed it when she was fussing with the pizza. When he'd first arrived, she'd been her usual warm, happy self. She'd joked with him as though she hadn't a care in the world.

Cody frowned. Since the afternoon of their picnic when they'd gotten caught in the downpour, Cody had noticed subtle changes in her. She seemed more spontaneous, more open with him.

He was willing to admit there'd been numerous intricate transformations in their relationship over the past ten days. They'd spent hours together, getting to know each other, growing to love each other.

And for most of that time, Cody had to struggle to keep his hands off her.

He found himself studying her at every opportunity, and whenever he did he liked what he saw. She captivated him. When they were alone together, he'd learned how dangerous it was to kiss her — and how difficult it was to stop. She'd press her soft body against his, and it was a test by fire of his limited control.

In the distance Cody heard the anxiety in her voice as her phone conversation with the other man continued. Not wanting to listen in, Cody opened the screen door and walked outside, carrying the baby. He sat on the top step and let his gaze wander across the acres of prime pastureland.

"See all those pesky cattle, Eric?" he whispered to the baby held securely against his shoulder. "It'll all belong to you someday. Take some advice, though, boy . . ." He was about to tell Russ's son not to get involved with women because all they did was cause a man grief.

But he stopped himself. Christy hadn't caused him grief or trouble. If anything, she'd brought him the truest joy he'd ever felt. He hadn't realized how lonely he was. Nor had he known how isolated his life had become until she'd walked into it, bold as could be.

Okay, he mused, sighing deeply. He was in love. It wasn't supposed to happen, but it had. Damned if he knew what to do next. For a man in his thirties he'd had precious little experience with it. The one other time he'd committed his heart to a woman, it had cost him dearly. He hadn't been willing to place himself at risk again. Not until he met Christy.

Fifteen minutes passed before Christy finally joined him. He heard her moving behind him in the kitchen and felt the swish of the screen door as it opened.

"That was James," she said as she sat down on the step beside him.

"I heard." He didn't mean to be, but he

sounded flippant, uncaring.

"He . . . he's called two other times."

"That's none of my business," he informed her curtly.

"I know, but I want to be honest with you. Are you angry?"

"No."

"You sound angry."

"I'm not." And pigs fly, he told himself.

For a long moment Christy didn't say anything. She sat there looking like an angel, smelling like something out of a rose garden. How was a man supposed to resist her when she gazed at him with those large blue eyes of hers?

"I . . . almost told him about you. It was on the tip of my tongue to try to explain. But James seemed so preoccupied. He was visiting my parents, and I spoke to them, too, and . . ." She shrugged. "It was impossible."

"Why's that?" He made a determined effort to take the starch out of his voice.

She hesitated before answering. "My mom and dad like James a lot."

"I'm sure he's perfect son-in-law material."

Christy ignored that comment, which was probably best. He knew he wasn't dealing with this situation well. In fact, he was making a real jackass of himself.

"Now . . . now that I've had these two weeks with you, I think I accepted his proposal more to please my parents than because I was in love with James."

"I see." Several questions popped into his mind. Christy was a kind person, affectionate and empathetic, someone who tried to please others. Her parents, James, *him*.

"They like Russ, too," she hurried to add.

Cody didn't know what that proved, and frankly he wasn't in the frame of mind to ask.

"Or at least they do now. At first —" She stopped abruptly, as if she'd already said too much.

Cody didn't doubt that the week to come, when she confronted James and her family, would be one of the most difficult of her life. If she went through with it, if she decided to break off the engagement, after all.

"I . . . can't bear for us to spend our last night together arguing," she whispered.

Cody forced himself to relax. He couldn't bear it, either. He lifted his free arm and placed it around her shoulders, drawing her closer to him and Eric. She turned and smiled shyly up at him. With unhurried ease he lowered his head until their mouths met.

The kiss was long and slow and when he raised his head, Cody felt dizzy with yearning.

"Oh, Cody," she moaned, her fingers clutching his shirt collar, her eyes closed. "I hate to leave you."

He hated it, too, feared it more than he'd feared anything. He dreaded the moment she'd drive away from him.

Fear and dread. Fighting those emotions wasn't how he wanted to spend their last hours together.

"Are you sure you haven't forgotten anything?" Taylor asked for the tenth time. They stood beside Christy's car, Taylor in her housecoat, Christy in her traveling clothes — a comfortable pair of faded jeans and a long-sleeved T-shirt.

"I'm positive I've got everything." She'd checked the house twice, and even if she'd inadvertently left something behind, she'd be back. Soon, she hoped. As soon as she could clear up the situation with James. As soon as she was free.

Taylor hugged her, and Russ stepped forward, holding Eric. He placed his free arm around Christy and squeezed tight.

"Drive carefully," Taylor said, "and phone the minute you arrive in Seattle. You know

I'll worry until I hear from you." Tears brimmed from her sister's eyes as she reached for Christy one last time. "I really hate to see you go."

"I'll phone," Christy promised. As for the part about hating to leave, that went without saying.

"Where's Cody?" Russ asked, frowning.

"He's got the day shift," Christy explained. Although she'd spent until the wee hours of the morning saying goodbye to the sheriff, she half expected Cody to come barreling down the driveway before she headed out.

"Be a good little baby," she whispered to Eric, kissing his brow. "Remember your Aunt Christy." With no more reason to delay, she opened her car door and climbed inside.

As she was driving toward the road, Christy looked in the rearview mirror and caught sight of Taylor slipping her arm around her husband's waist. She rested her head on his broad chest and leaned against him, as though she needed his strength, his support.

The scene was a touching one, and Christy found herself blinking back tears.

She was still sniffling as she headed for the highway that would connect her with the interstate. It would be a straight shot to

Seattle after that.

Christy planned to make the best time she could. The sooner she got home, the sooner she could set her life in order.

Reaching across the seat, she located the thermos of coffee Taylor had insisted she take with her. Holding it between her legs, she struggled to unscrew the cap. It was difficult to do with one hand. She'd just about given up when a flashing blue and red light was reflected in her rearview mirror.

Cody.

Christy eased to the side of the road, turned off the engine and threw open the door. It was impossible to hold her emotions at bay a moment longer.

Her gaze was blurred with tears, but it didn't matter. Cody had come to her.

By the time she'd climbed out of her car, he was out of his. Not waiting for an invitation, she rushed toward him, sobbing, so grateful he'd come.

He caught her, encircling her waist with his arms and lifting her from the ground. His lips found hers, their mouths connecting with such force that it threw her head back. Christy didn't mind; she was as needy as Cody. As hungry. As lost.

He continued to kiss her, saying with his body what he couldn't with words. That he loved her, needed her and was desperately afraid of losing her.

Christy understood and responded to each doubt.

"There's a side road about two miles back. Do you know where I mean?"

She nodded, remembered having driven past it minutes earlier.

"Meet me there?"

"Yes."

By the time she climbed back into her car, Christy was trembling from the inside out. Her stomach felt tight, and her heart was pounding. Cody made a U-turn and led the way. Christy followed willingly.

He pulled onto the dirt road, stirring up layers of fine dust, partially obliterating his vehicle. He drove past a wide curve, then he parked at the side. Christy watched as he reached for his radio. She got out of her car and waited for him.

"I told dispatch I wouldn't be available for the next fifteen minutes," he explained, his dark eyes holding hers. "I know it's not long enough to say what I want to say, but it's all the time I dare take."

Christy nodded.

He brushed his fingertips over her damp cheek. "You've been crying."

"I . . . couldn't get the thermos open."

"That's why?" he asked softly.

"No, of course it's not. I don't want to go. Oh, Cody, it's so much harder to leave you than I thought it would be." She tried unsuccessfully to swallow a sob.

"Don't cry," Cody pleaded. He held her against his chest and lowered his head. When he kissed her, it was with desperation and urgency, his mouth slanting over hers. She clung to him, giving as much as she took.

He kissed her neck, nuzzled it. Christy let her head fall back, allowing him to do whatever he wished. She was his for this moment, this hour, this day.

His warm mouth skimmed the length of her throat, planting moist kisses along her shoulder blade . . . then lower, much lower.

Slowly, as if he was calling upon all the self-control he possessed, Cody raised his head. "Letting you go is the hardest thing I've ever done," he whispered. He smoothed the hair away from her face and kissed her again.

A well-modulated voice came over the radio of the patrol car, reminding them both who and what Cody was. A man who'd pledged to serve and protect. As much as he would've liked to stay with her, the time had come for them to return to their separate lives.

"I'll follow you to the county line," he told her. He held open her car door, looking very much like the dignified sheriff he was. There was little evidence of the loving interlude that had passed between them.

A nod was all Christy could manage. She slid into the driver's seat. Her hand closed around the key. Cody held on to her door, his eyes trained directly ahead.

"I guess this is goodbye," she said hoarsely. "At least for now."

He nodded. "For now. You'll drive carefully?"

"Of course."

Again he nodded, closed her door and then stepped back. He seemed about to say something else, but then changed his mind.

Christy waited for him to enter his patrol car before starting her engine. She sent him a smile and glanced in her rearview mirror as she entered the main road.

True to his word, Cody followed her for several miles. In the distance she read the sign that stated she was leaving Custer County. An immediate knot formed in her throat, making it difficult to swallow.

Her rearview mirror showed Cody's red and blue lights flashing. She pulled over and stopped. Cody eased the patrol car in behind her.

He was out of his vehicle before she had a chance to free her seat belt. Lowering her window, she looked at him expectantly.

"One last thing before you go." His voice was deep and gravelly. "I love you, Christy. Come back to me."

EIGHT

"James," Christy said quietly, "you know I consider you one of my dearest friends. I've always heard good friends make the best husbands . . . no," she mumbled, her hands tightening around the steering wheel. "That doesn't sound right. Think, Christy, think!"

She'd just crossed the Idaho-Washington border and was within six hours of Seattle and home. Every mile, every minute, led her closer to the confrontation with James and her parents.

For the past two days Christy had carefully rehearsed what she planned to say, outlining her speech, inordinately conscious of each word.

James would be devastated, her parents shocked.

When it came right down to it, Christy was more worried about confronting her parents than she was James, especially her father, whom she adored. Eric Manning always seemed to think he knew what was best for her; for the most part, Christy had agreed with him. And he'd decided James would be the perfect husband for his youngest daughter.

The hours sped past, far too quickly to suit Christy. As she approached the outskirts of Seattle she found that she was traveling well below the speed limit, which produced several heated stares from her fellow travelers.

Once she'd arrived at her apartment building and had unloaded her car, Christy paced her living room restlessly. She'd assumed that once she was surrounded by everything that was familiar, some of the uneasiness would leave her.

It didn't. In fact, she was more agitated now than ever.

Gathering her courage, she decided to call her family and deal with them first. She planned to ask if it was convenient for her to come over, hoping it would be. The she could quickly put an end to this madness.

Once she was alone with her parents, she'd tell them she intended to break her engagement. Her argument was prepared, her decision unshakable.

Her first choice would've been to do it over the phone, but that would be the cowardly way out. Her only option was to confront them together. Once that was finished she'd go and see James.

As she reached for her phone, her stomach tensed. She wasn't sure what to expect from her parents or James and tried not to dwell on how they'd react to her news. She closed her eyes and prayed someone would answer before she lost her courage and hung up the phone.

"Hello."

"Jason?" He was her second-oldest brother and the handsomest of the lot, or so he liked to claim. At thirty-two he was a "catch," only he enjoyed playing the field far too much to settle down with any one woman.

"Christy? When did you get back?"

"Just a few minutes ago." How odd she sounded. Christy prayed Jason wouldn't notice. "What are you doing there? Are Mom and Dad around?"

"I'm here 'cause I took the day off. Mom and Dad are out but they'll be back any minute." He paused. "You don't know yet, do you?"

"Know what?" Jason loved playing games, dangling bits of information in front of her like bait, making her hungry for more.

"Never mind."

"Jason, I've been on the road for two days,

and to be frank, I'm not up to any of your trick questions." Under normal circumstances Christy would have been amused and played along, but not now.

"Hey, sweetie, no trick questions with this one. All I can say is you have a real surprise waiting for you. Mom's slaved every day since you've been gone, so if I were you, I'd make my presence known soon."

"Thank you so much," Christy muttered sarcastically. "Talking to you is like looking through a telescope with the lens cap on."

"Always happy to oblige," Jason responded with a light chuckle. "Just drop by the house soon. . . . In fact, the sooner the better."

Christy intended on doing exactly that. "I'll be over in fifteen minutes. By the way, how's Mom?" Breaking her leg had kept Elizabeth Manning at home for several weeks, and Christy knew how terribly disappointed her mother had been about missing this important time with her eldest daughter and newborn grandson.

"Mom's doing great. Especially now . . ." He didn't finish the enigmatic statement, and Christy refused to fall into his hands by asking what he meant. "If you don't mind, I'll stick around for a while, too. I'd like to get a look at your face once you find out what's been going on around here. Mom's in seventh heaven. At the rate things are going, you're likely to end up in one of those celebrity magazines."

"Cute, Jason, very cute." Christy had no idea what he was talking about, but that was typical of her older brother. Over the last few years, his comments had taken on a biting edge. Christy didn't know what his problem was, but she wished he'd straighten out whatever was wrong.

In an attempt to delay the unavoidable, Christy played back the messages on her answering machine while she leafed through two weeks' worth of mail. Anyone who mattered wouldn't have phoned because they'd know she was out of town, but she couldn't help being curious.

There were several beeps, indicating that whoever had called had hung up before leaving a message. Probably salesmen.

Deciding it was a waste of time, Christy started for her front door when Taylor's voice, hesitant and unsure, came over the tinny speaker. "Christy, call me as soon as you get home. Something's come up that we need to discuss."

There was an uncharacteristic note in her sister's voice, an uncertainty that suggested something was terribly amiss.

Puzzled, Christy returned to the phone

163

and placed a long-distance call to Cougar Point. Mandy answered, sounding as cheerful as ever.

"Taylor's not here," Russ's sister explained. "She drove into Miles City for Eric's first appointment with the pediatrician. Do you want me to have her call you once she gets back? I don't think it'll be too much longer. I know she was anxious to talk to you."

"No. I'm headed to my parents' house now. I'll phone again later." Hopefully by that time everything would be settled. She could contact Taylor and Russ and then talk to Cody. The mere thought of him made her go weak. Seemingly by accident they'd found each other and unexpectedly discovered what it meant to fall in love. Neither of them had been looking for this, neither of them fully understood why it had happened, but it was right. Right for Cody. Right for Christy.

After two long days on the road, she was physically exhausted and mentally depleted. She'd considered delaying this confrontation until she was well-rested and relaxed, but she knew she couldn't do that. The engagement to James hung over her head and she wouldn't find peace until all the obstacles were cleared out out of the road that would lead her back to her sheriff.

Her parents' luxury vehicle was in the driveway when Christy drove up. Jason's car was in the street, and Christy parked her own behind his. Even before she'd turned off the engine, her father had opened the front door and was walking toward her, arms outstretched.

Eric Manning embraced his daughter, hugging her tight. From the time she was little Christy had always felt a special closeness to her parents. Most of her friends had rebelled in one way or another against their families, but never Christy. She'd never felt the need.

"When did you get back?" her father asked.

"Not even half an hour ago." She slipped her arm around his thickening waist and they walked toward the sprawling brick house. The lawn was a soft, lush green. Many a happy hour had been spent racing across this very same grass. Echoes of her childhood laughter seemed to mock her now.

Elizabeth Manning stood in the entryway, her left leg encased from her foot to just below her knee in a hot pink cast. She broke into a broad smile as Christy approached the front door.

"Sweetheart, it's so good to have you home."

"It's good to be home, and before you ask, yes, I brought tons of pictures of Eric."

"Oh, that's wonderful, I can't tell you how excited we are that Russ and Taylor named him after your father."

Christy stepped into the house. It was a large home built into a hill overlooking the freeway that cut a wide path through the heart of Seattle. The basement opened onto an enormous, landscaped yard with a profusion of flower beds and space for a vegetable garden, whose bounty spilled over to friends and neighbors every summer.

"How's the leg?"

"Better," Elizabeth said, dismissing her daughter's concern with a quick shake of her head. She was walking with a cane now, leaning heavily upon it. Christy knew her mother well enough to realize Elizabeth Manning would never want to burden her children with the fact that she was in pain. But her mother did look much healthier, Christy mused. The sparkle was back in her eyes, and a flush of excitement glowed from her cheeks. Christy couldn't remember how long it'd been since she'd seen her mother so happy. No doubt the birth of their third grandson was responsible.

"You're looking terrific," Christy said, kissing her mother's cheek.

"Actually, sweetie, we have you to thank for that," her father murmured, sharing an enigmatic smile with wife.

"Me?" Apparently they were playing the same game as Jason.

"Eric, let's not discuss this in the entryway."

Her father chuckled, and Christy noted that his eyes seemed brighter, too. He certainly was in one of his better moods. Christy would like to think it was all due to her arrival and the fact that she'd brought pictures of their grandson. But somehow she doubted it, especially after having spoken to Jason.

Her second-oldest brother was sitting in the family room in front of the television when Christy walked in. He was wearing a Seattle Mariners baseball cap, which he had on much of the time.

"Welcome home, little sister," he greeted her. He stood and hugged her, then stepped back, wiggling his eyebrows.

"All right, you guys," Christy said, claiming the easy chair next to Jason. "What's going on around here?"

Her father's mouth started to quiver, as though he was having difficulty holding back his excitement. He shared another look with his wife of thirty-five years.

"If you'll recall, your mother's spirits were low after she fell and broke her leg. Missing out on this special time with Taylor and Russ depressed her."

"I didn't even realize how melancholy I'd become until Eric mentioned it," Elizabeth said. "Sometimes I swear he knows me better than I know myself."

Christy felt herself nod.

"Your father's the one who came up with the idea for an engagement party."

"An . . . engagement party," Christy echoed, coming halfway out of her chair, appalled and dismayed.

Her mother pressed her fingers to her lips, almost giddy with delight. "We knew you'd be pleased."

"I . . . I . . ." Christy was at a complete loss for words. Somehow she managed a smile and slumped back into the cushions of the overstuffed chair.

"You can't imagine what fun we've had," Elizabeth continued, her voice animated. "I'm afraid your father got carried away. He insisted we order the best of everything. We've rented the Eagles Hall, got the invitations mailed — engraved ones. Oh, sweetie, I can hardly wait for you to see them. We spent hour after hour with the caterers. I can't even *begin* to tell you what a fabulous time I — we — had planning every detail of this party. I can't help feeling proud of everything we accomplished in such a short time."

"It was just what your mother needed," Christy's father inserted smoothly, looking equally delighted. "Elizabeth's been like a kid again from the moment we decided to go through with this."

"I see." Christy went completely numb. It seemed impossible that no one was aware of it.

"I suppose we're a pair of old fools, but when Taylor married Russ in Reno, your father and I felt cheated out of a large family wedding. We've been looking forward to throwing one for years."

"When?" It was torture getting the word past the tightness that all but blocked her throat.

"That's the crazy part," Jason told her. "Mom and Dad put this entire thing together in two weeks."

Christy still didn't understand; not much of the conversation made sense. Her look must have conveyed her confusion.

"The party's tomorrow night," Elizabeth said, her face radiating her excitement.

"Tomorrow night?"

"I know it sounds crazy, and we took a chance booking it so close to the end of your vacation, but there were only a few dates available at the Eagles Hall, and it was either tomorrow night or three months from now."

"In fact, the only reason we were able to get the hall is because of a last-minute cancellation," Eric said. "I had no idea we'd need to book this sort of thing so far in advance."

"James?" No one seemed to notice she was having trouble speaking, which Christy supposed was a blessing of sorts.

"He knows, of course, but we decided to keep it a secret for you. A welcome-home surprise."

Christy nodded, hating the way she continued to sit in her parents' home, saying nothing when it felt as if the foundations of her world were crumbling at her feet. Her mother and father and Jason were all looking at her, waiting for some response, but for the life of her, Christy couldn't give them one.

Her eyes met with her brother's.

He winked broadly. "Mom and Dad are sparing no expense. If the wedding's half as elaborate as the engagement party, then your big day's going to be spectacular."

Eric Manning chuckled. "It isn't every father who has a daughter as special as Christy."

Christy forced a smile although she longed to stand up and beg them to put an end to this craziness. She didn't love James. She loved Cody. She couldn't possibly go through with an engagement to a man she didn't intend to marry.

She glanced from her mother to her father, both of them staring at her with bright, eager smiles, as though waiting for her to burst into a song of praise for their efforts.

"I . . . I . . ." The words froze on her lips.

"Honey, look," Elizabeth murmured devotedly to her husband. "Christy's speechless. Oh, sweetie, you don't need to say anything. Your father and I understand. If anyone should be giving thanks, it's me. I was so miserable after my fall. Planning this party was the best thing in the world for me. I've loved every minute of it. Keeping it a surprise has been so much fun."

There had to be a plausible excuse she could use to avoid this farce of an engagement party. "I don't have a dress." The words escaped her lips almost as quickly as they formed in her mind.

"Not to worry," Elizabeth said, her eyes glowing even brighter. "I thought of everything, if I do say so myself. I went shopping the other day and picked out a dress for you. If you don't like it, or it doesn't fit, we can exchange it first thing in the morning."

First thing in the morning. The words echoed in her ears. "I . . . I'm supposed to go back to work." That sounded reasonable to her. After two weeks away from the law firm, Christy was expected back. They needed her. They were short-staffed without her. She couldn't demand additional time off to exchange a party dress.

"No need to worry about that, either," Eric said. "James has that covered. He talked it over with the office manager, and she's given you two extra days off with pay."

"Tomorrow, of course, will be filled with all the last-minute details for the party," Elizabeth rattled on, rubbing her palms together.

"You didn't tell Taylor?" Her older sister would've said something to her; Christy was sure of it.

"Well, not right away. I mailed her a long letter and an invitation so it would arrive the day you were scheduled to leave Montana. I'm guessing she has it by now. I couldn't take the chance of mailing it any sooner for fear you'd find it, and I didn't want to say anything when we phoned in case she inadvertently let the cat out of the bag. I wanted to keep this a surprise."

"I see," Christy murmured.

"Your father and I don't expect Taylor to fly home for the party, not so soon after having the baby. She and Russ will come out for the wedding. Which is something else we need to discuss. Talk to James, sweetie — the sooner we have a date, the better. There's so much to do, and I so want this wedding to be carefully planned. I can't tell you how much I've learned in the past two weeks. Right after the party tomorrow night, we're going to sit down and discuss the wedding."

Christy nodded, simply because she lacked the courage to explain there would never be a wedding, at least not one in which James was the bridegroom.

"You are surprised, aren't you?" Jason demanded, looking exceptionally cocky, as though he was the person responsible for pulling this whole affair together.

Surprise was too mild a word for what Christy was experiencing. Even shock and dismay were too mild.

Horror and panic more aptly described her feelings.

James! She needed to talk to James. He'd help her. He'd understand, and then together they'd clear up this mess. Together they could confront her parents and make *them* understand.

She stood before she realized what she was doing. Everyone in the room seemed to be staring holes straight through her. Glancing around, she offered them each a weak smile.

Always dutiful. Always obedient. Never causing a concern or a problem. Christy was about to destroy her good-girl image.

But first she had to talk to James.

Two messages were waiting for Christy on her answering machine when she returned late that afternoon. The first was from Cody and the second from Taylor.

Christy didn't answer either.

Instead she sat in her living room, staring into space, weighed down by guilt, pressured beyond anything she'd ever experienced and entangled in circumstances beyond her control.

How long she stayed there Christy didn't know. Here she was safe. Here she was protected. Here she could hide.

That small sense of security, however, quickly disintegrated. Knowing there was nothing else she could do to stop the progression of events, she stood and walked into the kitchen. She paused in front of the phone, then abruptly picked it up before she had a change of heart.

Cody wasn't home, and she left an all-too-brief message. Her next call was to Taylor.

"Christy, what's going on?" Taylor burst out the instant she recognized her younger sister. "I got this crazy letter from Mom about a surprise engagement party for you. What's happening?"

"You mean about the party?" Christy asked. Her voice lacked any level of emotion. She had none left.

"Of course I mean the party," Taylor cried. "Do you mean to say you're going through with it?"

"I don't have any choice."

"Christy, you can't be serious! What about Cody? I thought you were in love with him. I may be out of line here, but I could've sworn you . . ." She inhaled deeply. "I'd better stop before I say something I shouldn't. Just answer me one question. Do you or do you not love Cody Franklin?"

Christy wiped the tears from her face and nodded wildly. "You know I do."

"Then it seems to me you're allowing Mom and Dad to dictate your life."

"You don't understand," Christy whimpered.

"What's there to understand?"

"Mom broke her leg —" She couldn't go on, wondering if she should even try to describe this hopeless mess. Even if she did it was doubtful Taylor would understand.

"I know about Mom's accident," Taylor returned impatiently.

"She was terribly depressed afterward. I saw it, we all did, but apparently it didn't go away like everyone expected it would. Then Dad came up with the brilliant idea of planning this engagement party."

"Oh, dear."

"Mom put everything she had into it, and now —"

"Christy, I know it's difficult, but you've got to remember Mom and Dad planned this party without consulting you."

That was true enough, but it didn't change the facts. "I can't humiliate them. I thought if I talked to James, told him about Cody, everything would work out, but then I discovered I couldn't do that, either. I wanted us to face Mom and Dad and make some kind of decision together about the party, but that's impossible now. Everything's so crazy. . . . I can't believe this is happening."

"Do you mean to say James doesn't know about Cody yet?"

Christy closed her eyes.

"Christy?"

"I . . . couldn't tell him." She stiffened, waiting for the backlash of anger that was sure to follow.

After a short silence, Taylor said, "You *couldn't* tell James about Cody?"

The trouble she had forming the words was painfully obvious. "You heard me."

There was another silence. "I see."

"How could you possibly *see?*" Christy demanded, keeping her voice level, when she wanted to scream at the accusation she heard in her sister's voice. "I went to him, fully intending to tell him everything."

"Then why didn't you?"

"For two months James has been preparing for the most important trial of his career."

"You mean to say you're worried about James's *career?* At a time like this?"

Christy ignored her sister's outburst. "A businessman from Kirkland . . . You must know Alfred Mulligan. He's the one who does all those crazy television ads. Anyway, he's been charged with cheating on his taxes. The whole case is extremely complicated, and you know as well as I do how messy this kind of thing can get when the federal government is involved." She waited for Taylor to agree with her.

"What's that got to do with anything?"

Christy hated the angry impatience she heard in her sister's voice. It was all too clear that Taylor was upset with her. Christy felt Taylor's disapproval as strongly as a slap. All her life she'd experienced love and approval, especially from her family, and it hurt more than she could bear to feel such overwhelming censure from her only sister.

"You don't understand," Christy tried again. "James has been working day and night for weeks to get ready for this trial. It was scheduled for the first of next month, but he learned this afternoon they've called the case early. He's making the opening statement tomorrow morning."

"I'm afraid I don't understand the relevance of all this."

"I don't expect you to. James has worked himself into a frenzy. I've never seen him like this. So much hangs in the balance for him."

"That's fine, but I still don't —"

"He has a chance to win this case, but it's going to be difficult," Christy went on, cutting off her sister's protest. "James knows that. Everyone does, but if by some miracle he can pull this off, it could mean a partnership for him."

"Oh, Christy," Taylor said with a groan.

"If I broke off the engagement now, it could ruin everything for him."

"That's James's problem, not yours."

"Maybe it is his problem. I don't know anymore. I do know that I can't do this to him. Not on the eve of the most important trial of his career. Not when James has finally been given the chance to prove himself. If anything went wrong, I'd always blame myself."

The silence hummed as Taylor considered her words. "What about Cody?" she asked finally. "Have you given any thought to *his* feelings?"

"Yes." Christy had thought of little else. Never in her life had she asked more of a person than she was asking of Cody. Another woman had destroyed his trust, and there was nothing to assure Christy that he'd want anything to do with her after this.

As painful as it was, as difficult, she found she couldn't humiliate her parents and risk destroying James's chances with this case.

Even if it meant she lost Cody.

NINE

Something was wrong. Cody felt it instinctively, all the way to the marrow of his bones. Christy had left two separate messages on his answering machine, and every time he'd played them back, he'd felt an achy, restless sensation. It wasn't what she'd said, but how she'd said it. She sounded lighthearted and cheerful, but beneath the facade, Cody heard unmistakable confusion.

He'd tried to phone her back, but to no avail. Unable to sleep, he rose in the early morning hours and drove around the back roads outside town, trying to make sense of what was happening. Or not happening.

He couldn't find the answers, not when he didn't understand the questions.

His greatest fears were about to be realized. Once again he'd fallen in love, involved his life with a woman who couldn't be trusted.

Christy isn't Becca, his heart shouted, but Cody had virtually given up listening.

The sun had barely crested the hill as Cody sat in his Cherokee, looking at the valley below, pondering what he should do. If anything. Dammit all, he should never have let this go so far. Becca had taught him everything he needed to know about women and love.

Dawn burst over the hillside, with golden rays of sunlight splashed against the rugged landscape, and small patches of light on the horizon.

Cody released a jagged sigh, then started his car. As much as he'd like to turn his back on the entire situation and pretend the past two weeks with Christy hadn't happened, he knew the effort would be futile.

He glanced at his watch, knowing Russ and Taylor would be up and about. He needed to talk.

The light from the kitchen window glowed as Cody approached the ranch house. He pulled in to the yard, turned off the engine and waited until the door opened and Russ appeared on the back porch.

Climbing out of the car, Cody joined his friend.

"I thought that was you," Russ said, opening the door in mute invitation.

181

Cody removed his hat and set it on the peg while Russ walked over to the coffeepot and automatically poured him a mug.

"Taylor's feeding Eric," Russ said. "She'll be out in a few minutes."

Cody nodded and straddled a high-backed wooden chair.

Russ sat across from him. "Personally I don't think this thing with Christy is as bad as it sounds. Although, to be honest, if I was in your shoes, I don't know what I'd do."

Cody hadn't a clue what his friend was talking about but decided not to say anything, hoping Russ would explain without him having to ask.

"How're you holding up?"

"Fine." Cody was about to drop the charade and ask his friend what was going on when Taylor came in, wearing a long pink housecoat. Her hair was mussed and fell to the middle of her back. She offered Cody an apologetic smile, and once more he was left to interpret the meaning. His gut was tightening, and he didn't know how much longer he could go on pretending.

"Good morning, Cody," Taylor greeted him, helping herself to a cup of coffee. It seemed to Cody that her smile conveyed more concern than welcome.

It was all Cody could do not to leap to his feet and demand someone tell him what was happening.

"I suppose you're here to talk about Christy?" she asked gently. If Russ hadn't said a word, Cody would've guessed something was wrong just from the way Taylor was looking at him — as if she wanted to put her arms around him and weep.

"Christy's been on my mind," he answered brusquely.

"You realize she doesn't have any choice, don't you?" Taylor added. Her eyes, so like Christy's, appealed to him to be open-minded. "Russ and I've gone round and round about this and —"

"Any choice about what?" Cody demanded. His friends exchanged a surprised look.

"You mean Christy didn't get hold of you?"

"No."

"Then you don't know about the engagement party?"

"All I got was two messages in which she sounds like Mary Sunshine. I *knew* she wasn't telling me something. I sensed that right away."

It took a moment for the news to hit him. Engagement party? That meant she was still involved with . . . If he hadn't already been sitting down, Cody would have needed a chair fast. He'd heard of men who'd had their feet kicked out from under them, but he'd never understood the expression until then.

"Oh, dear." Taylor reached for her coffee and it was clear that she was upset. Her hands trembled, and her eyes avoided meeting his.

Cody transferred his attention to Russ, who looked as uncomfortable as his wife. "What's going on?" Cody asked in a deceptively calm voice.

Once more, husband and wife exchanged glances as if silently deciding between themselves who would do the talking. Apparently Russ presented his wife with the unpleasant task, because she swallowed, then turned to Cody. "My sister's caught in a series of difficult circumstances."

"What the hell does that mean?"

"Apparently my mother took the two weeks while Christy was here in Montana to plan an elaborate engagement party. It seems her spirts needed a boost, and my father thought involving her in planning a party would help. Unfortunately he was right. Mom threw herself into the project and arranged the event of the year, starring

Christy and James."

"Are you telling me she's going through with it?"

"She doesn't have much of a choice. The celebration's scheduled for this evening."

This second bit of information hit Cody with the same impact as the first. "You've got to be kidding!"

"I wish we were," Russ said, his expression annoyed. "My in-laws mean well, but Christy's trapped in this fiasco simply because there isn't time to cancel it now."

"What about James?" Cody asked, stiffening as he mentioned the other man's name. Every time he thought about the Seattle attorney, he struggled with anger and jealousy. James Wilkens had far more claim to Christy than he did. They both loved her, but it was James who'd given her an engagement ring. It was James her parents wanted her to marry.

"James is another problem," Taylor whispered.

Cody didn't understand. "You mean he's refusing to release her from the engagement?"

"He doesn't know Christy intends to break it off," Russ said without preamble.

Cody would've accepted just about anything more readily than he did this news.

Christy had played him for a fool, used him the same way Becca had, for her own selfish purposes — whatever they might be.

"She's going to tell James everything," Taylor said heatedly in her sister's defense.

Cody didn't bother to comment, still reeling from this last news.

"When I talked to her, she'd just returned from seeing James. She'd gone to him with the best of intentions, wanting to tell him about you and break off the engagement before it went any further. She was hoping the two of them could discuss the engagement party and decide what could be done."

"She didn't say a word about me to James, did she?" At Taylor's wilted look, Cody decided that was all he needed to know. He stood, emptied the contents of his mug into the sink and set it on the counter so hard that it almost shattered.

"She couldn't tell him," Taylor cried. "If you love Christy the way you claim, you'll listen long enough to find out why."

Cody did love Christy, but he didn't know how much more battering his heart and his pride could take. He stood frozen, waiting for Taylor to continue.

"If she told James about you, she might put his entire career in jeopardy." For the next ten minutes Russ and Taylor took turns explaining the situation as best they could.

"Christy doesn't have any choice but to follow through with this farce of a party, don't you see?"

Taylor did an admirable job of presenting her sister's case; Cody would give her that.

She kept her pleading eyes focused on him. "If it'd been up to her, she would've ended the engagement five minutes after she got home."

Cody didn't respond, although it was apparent his friends were waiting for him to say something.

"You've got to appreciate the situation Christy's in," Taylor went on. "What would *you* have done had the circumstances been reversed?"

Cody closed his eyes, pondering the dilemma. What would he do?

He just didn't know.

"Oh, sweetheart!" Christy's mother exclaimed, stepping back to examine the effect of the full-length layered blue dress. "You look like an angel. Eric, come and see."

Eric Manning, wearing a white tuxedo with a pale blue cummerbund the same shade as Christy's dress, stepped gingerly into the living room. He eyed his youngest daughter and nodded approvingly. "You make an old man proud," he said with a warm smile.

"You've never looked lovelier," her mother added.

Christy managed a smile. She had no idea how she was going to make it through this party. She might be able to fool her parents, but surely someone would notice. Rich would. Of her three brothers, she'd always been closest to Rich. He'd take one look at her and immediately guess that something was wrong.

Not that it would make any difference. She'd stand before family and friends and pretend to be madly in love with James, pretend to be an eager bride-to-be. But the only thing Christy was eager for at the moment was to put this evening behind her.

"I'd like to propose a toast to the happy couple, my sister Christy and the love of her life, James Wilkens." Rich Manning raised his champagne glass to the couple.

Christy grinned at her brother and fought the urge to empty her champagne glass over his head. Of all the guests, she'd expected him to realize how miserable she was. Instead, he'd unwittingly made things even worse.

Smiling faces nodded appreciatively at her brother's words before the party-goers sipped the vintage champagne. The round of toasts had been going on for several minutes. Christy wasn't sure how much more of this she could endure.

Her father had proposed the first toast, followed by her uncles and all three of her brothers. Each seemed to add something to the list of blessings they wished for her and James.

Christy swallowed another sip of champagne as her fiancé stood at her side, tall and debonair. She could barely look at him without being overwhelmed with guilt. They'd spent two hours in each other's company, and neither had spoken more than a handful of sentences.

In retrospect Christy wondered how she could possibly have agreed to spend the rest of her life with James. He was wonderful, but it was increasingly obvious that they were painfully mismatched.

Hoping she wasn't being conspicuous, Christy scanned the gathering, wondering if it was possible for anyone to read her thoughts. Not that it would do any good.

"Would you like something to eat?" James asked, glancing toward the linen-draped tables where trays of hors d'oeuvres lay waiting.

Christy shook her head, positive she wouldn't be able to keep down a single bite. "Nothing for me, thanks. What about you?"

"I'm fine," James answered.

The music started, and a handful of couples were making their way to the gleaming wooden floor. "I've always been terrible at this sort of thing," James confessed, reaching for Christy's hand. "But I suppose it's expected of us."

Christy nodded, wanting nothing more than to escape. A path was cleared as James led her to the dance floor and slipped his arm around her waist, careful to maintain a respectable distance between them. The music was slow and melodious, a love ballad, whose words seemed to ridicule her more than anything that had preceded the dancing.

James smiled into Christy's eyes as they moved across the floor. Soon other couples joined them.

Her fiancé seemed to relax a little more now that they weren't the only two on the floor. For that matter so did Christy. "I'm sorry I haven't been myself this evening," James murmured regretfully.

Christy was ashamed to admit she hadn't

noticed. Her whole attention had been focused on simply getting through this ordeal.

"The Mulligan case is going to take up a lot of my time over the next few weeks, and I can only hope you'll be patient with me."

Christy was horrified to realize she'd forgotten all about the trial and how important it was to him. "Oh, James, I'm so sorry. I didn't even ask how everything went this morning."

"Not as well as I'd hoped," he mumbled under his breath.

"I'm sorry," she said again. "But I understand you're going to be busy. In fact, it might actually work out for the best. You see, I met —" She wasn't allowed to finish.

"I knew you'd be understanding," he said, cutting her off. He smiled gently and drew her toward him. "You always have been."

"You, too," she whispered sarcastically, but James didn't respond.

Closing her eyes, she tried to pretend it was Cody's arms around her. That was the only way she'd be able to continue this farce. Keeping his image in her mind gave her a sense of purpose, a means of enduring this disastrous night.

After a respectable number of dances, James escorted her off the floor. Until then

Christy hadn't noticed how tired and defeated he looked. Several family members insisted on dances with her, and Christy found herself on the floor with a number of uncles, her brothers and longtime family friends.

James was doing his duty, as well, keeping the women from both families occupied. She did see that he managed to do so without dancing with any of them, and that made her smile, however briefly.

It wasn't until the end of the evening, when Christy decided she just might survive, that her aunt Lois, her mother's youngest sister, asked the impossible question. "When's the date for the wedding?"

The whole room went silent. The music ceased, and everyone turned to stare at Christy and James. They were sitting together in a long row of folding chairs against the wall. It was the first time they'd sat down that evening.

Christy felt like a cornered animal. The cracker in her mouth seemed to go down her throat whole.

"You don't have an engagement party without letting those you love know when you're planning the wedding," Aunt Lois said.

James glanced at Christy. "We haven't had

a chance to discuss a date, have we, darling?"

"No," Christy muttered. It wouldn't look good to announce that she was counting the days until she could break the engagement. If she was going to discuss a wedding date with anyone, it would be with Cody. But he hadn't asked her, and after he learned about this evening, Christy doubted he'd ever want to see her again.

"Springtime is always lovely for a wedding." Aunt Lois stood directly in front of her, waving her arms, demanding the attention of Christy and everyone else. "George and I were married in May, and the flowers were gorgeous." Pressing her gloved hands together, she released a slow sigh of remembered happiness.

"But May's almost a year away," Elizabeth Manning objected loudly, walking across the dance floor to join this all-important discussion. "Why wait so long? I was thinking more along the lines of November."

"November?" Christy echoed.

"The leaves are always so pretty then. You know how I love orange, brown and yellow," she said, looking at her daughter.

Already Christy could see her mother's mind working, plotting and planning. She'd enjoyed making the arrangements for the engagement party so much that she couldn't wait to start on all the pomp and ceremony of a formal wedding.

"With your dark coloring, Christy, an autumn theme would be perfect."

"Personally I favor a December wedding," Eric Manning shouted. He'd obviously had more than his share of champagne.

"December?" Elizabeth shrieked, shaking her head. "Never."

"All right," Eric countered. "Let's ask Christy and James which date they prefer. This is, after all, their wedding."

"Ah." Christy couldn't think. Her mind froze along with her hands, which were raised halfway to her mouth, her fingers clutching a delicate artichoke canapé. In a panic she looked at James, her eyes wide in speechless appeal. If ever she needed rescuing, it was now.

"What do you say, sweetheart?" her mother asked.

By some miracle Christy managed to lower the cracker to her plate. "I . . . I haven't given the matter much thought."

"When George and I decided to marry, we couldn't do it fast enough," Aunt Lois informed the group.

"November," James said decisively. "Your

aunt's right. There's no need to put off the wedding."

"We don't have to choose a date *now,* do we?" Christy asked. "Not when you're so busy with the Mulligan case."

His hand patted hers gently. "This trial will be over soon enough, and I've been selfish not to consider your feelings. Naturally you and your mother will want to start making all the necessary arrangements."

"November would be perfect." Elizabeth Manning opened her purse and withdrew a small appointment calendar. "Let's pick the date right now. How does the twelfth sound?"

Once more Christy found herself speechless. "Ah . . ."

"The twelfth sounds grand," James said triumphantly, and lightly touched his lips to Christy's cheek. "Isn't that right, darling?"

The whole world came to an abrupt halt, awaiting Christy's reply. The walls seemed to be falling in around her, until she could hardly breathe.

"Christy?" her mother probed, eyeing her curiously. "November 12 would be a beautiful day for a wedding, don't you agree?"

Cody slowly patrolled the deserted streets of Cougar Point, but his mind wasn't on the job. The crime wave of the century could be happening before his very eyes, and Cody doubted he would've noticed.

How could he? The only reason he'd agreed to take this shift was in an effort to forget that Christy was with James tonight.

While Cody dutifully served his constituents, Christy was sipping champagne with her attorney fiancé. No doubt his diamond was firmly placed on her ring finger and she was having the time of her life.

It hurt.

The pain was as real as anything he'd ever endured. Except that it hurt more. There wasn't a thing he could do to alter the chain of events that had led Christy into this predicament. Apparently there wasn't much she could do, either.

He tried to remind himself that the woman he loved would go to great lengths not to hurt others, even if it meant hurting herself. But Christy wasn't the only one suffering.

Cody felt like a casualty of circumstance. And there was nothing he could do. . . .

It was late when he rolled into the station — after eleven. He got out of the patrol car and saw Russ's pickup truck parked out front. Frowning, he made his way inside.

Russ Palmer unfolded his long legs and stood. "About time you got here."

"Problems?"

Russ nodded. "A few. I thought it might be a good idea if we talked."

The anxiety that had been following him around all night grew more intense. "I'll meet you in ten minutes."

Since the bowling alley was the only restaurant in town that stayed open this late, Cody didn't need to mention where they'd meet.

Russ was already in the booth, holding a white ceramic mug, when Cody walked inside. Cody slid in across from him, wondering how his friend had come to pick the same booth he'd sat in with Christy. He'd been in love with her then and hadn't even known it.

"What's so all-fired important to bring you out this time of night?" Cody asked.

"Taylor."

That didn't explain a lot.

The cook brought out a second mug for Cody and returned to the kitchen. Russ stared after the other man.

"You don't mean Taylor, you mean Christy, right?"

Russ nodded glumly.

"What did she do now? Run off with Gypsies? Marry the garbageman?"

"Worse."

"I suppose this has to do with the engagement party."

Once more Russ nodded. "Apparently no one guessed her real feelings. It seems everyone was too concerned about how much liquor made it into the punch bowl to ask Christy how *she* felt about the whole thing."

"I should be grateful for that?"

"No," Russ answered. "She went through the evening like a real trooper. She loves her family, and she did this for their sake, but she didn't like it."

"She's not the only one."

"I can well imagine," Russ said with a sympathetic sigh. "I know how I'd feel in the circumstances."

"I'm not sure what to do anymore." Cody rubbed his face wearily. "Tell me what happened. I can deal with that better than not knowing."

Russ seemed uncertain where to begin.

"Just spit it out," Cody said, trying to persuade himself he should forget he'd ever met Christy Manning.

"She's sick. Started throwing up at the party. Taylor talked to her and said Christy's in pretty rough shape."

For all his effort to portray disinterest, Cody's heart raced at the news. "What's

198

wrong?"

"It's not what you think."

"If she's feeling as bad as you say, then why didn't she contact me?"

"She's been trying to reach you for two days."

"I've been busy. What was I supposed to do? Phone her and suggest she enjoy her engagement party? I have some pride left, and frankly I'm holding on to it."

"She needs to talk to you. Call her."

Cody shrugged.

"If you've been avoiding her, don't. She doesn't deserve this. Not now."

"I've tried phoning," Cody confessed, as if admitting to a shortcoming in his character. "She's never there."

"You didn't leave a message?"

"No," he answered reluctantly. What was there to say in a message that would help their situation? As far as he could see, nothing.

"She's at her apartment now. Take my advice and put each other out of this misery. Talk to her."

Ten minutes later Cody unlocked his front door, turned on the light and walked into his living room. He scowled at the phone — but he didn't know who he was trying to kid. He practically lunged at it, he was so hungry for the sound of Christy's voice.

He dialed the Seattle number Russ had given him, and Christy answered even before the first ring had finished.

"Cody?" Her voice caught on his name before he had a chance to speak.

"Hello, Christy," he said in a voice that, to his own ears, sounded stiff and cold.

"Thank you for calling me."

Before he could respond, she asked, "Did Taylor tell you?"

"Tell me what?"

"What happened at the party."

"No." There was more? "Russ came into town and asked me to call you. He alluded to something but never said exactly what. Go ahead and tell me."

A slight hesitation followed. "I . . . it isn't easy."

"Dammit, Christy, what's going on now?" The possibilities that came to mind did little to put him at ease.

"I want to be honest with you," she said, her voice shaking. "I . . ." She paused, and Cody could hear her drag a deep breath through her lungs. "Something happened at the party tonight . . . something I never intended."

Cody wanted to come across as nonchalant, but he couldn't. He expelled his breath, trying to think of what she might have done that would make him stop loving her.

Nothing. She could do nothing. Even if she were to inform him that she'd given in to the pressure and married James that very night, it wouldn't be enough. He'd still love her. He'd always love her.

"November 12," she whispered.

"I beg your pardon?" She'd gone from guessing games to riddles.

"The wedding's set for November 12."

Ten

Christy rolled over and glanced at the illuminated dial of her clock radio. It was 10:00 a.m.

This was supposed to be her first day back at the office, but she'd had to phone in sick. A flu bug was what she'd told Marcia, the office manager, who was sympathetic enough to suggest Christy stay home. But it wasn't the flu that was making her ill.

It was something else entirely. Christy was heartsick, afraid she'd lost Cody forever. She felt trapped, doing what was right for everyone but herself.

Now she was wide awake, and the day stretched out before her. She could occupy herself with mindless game shows on television, but that would only use up an hour or two. Reading would help pass the time — if she could concentrate. She might even give some thought to phoning Cody.

No.

That was out of the question. Cody didn't want to talk to her, not anymore. She'd said everything she could to make him understand her predicament two nights earlier. The conversation had gone reasonably well until she'd told him she'd been forced to set a date for the wedding.

An unexpected sob tore through her throat, and fresh tears flooded her eyes. She'd done a lot of weeping over the past days. Damp, crumpled tissues lay scattered across her bedspread where she'd carelessly discarded them.

She loved Cody, and nothing she'd been able to say had convinced him of that. Cody, being a sheriff, saw life in terms of black and white. Either she'd agreed to the wedding date or she hadn't. Unfortunately Christy had sanctioned November 12, more or less, when pressured by James and her entire family. As soon as she confessed as much, her telephone conversation with Cody had ended abruptly.

She'd pleaded with him for understanding, tried to assure him she'd never willingly marry James, but it hadn't helped. They'd hung up with Cody promising to contact her after he'd had time to think.

Nearly thirty-four hours had passed. Surely he'd had adequate opportunity to come to some kind of decision.

The doorbell chimed, and sniffling, Christy reached for another tissue. She blew her nose before tossing aside her covers and climbing out of bed. She intended to send her visitor, whoever it was, away. She was in no mood for company.

With her luck, it was probably her mother wanting to discuss color schemes for the bridesmaids' dresses. If her car hadn't been parked directly in front of her door, she wouldn't even bother answering.

"Who is it?" she asked, squinting through the peephole and seeing no one.

"Cody Franklin."

"Cody . . . oh, Cody." Christy threw open the door. For one wild second she did nothing but stare into his wonderful face, convinced he'd been conjured up by her imagination. Before another second could pass, she launched herself into his arms.

Cody dropped his suitcase, clasping her around the waist with both arms. He hauled her to him with joyful abandon. Their mouths met in a kiss so fierce, it threatened to steal her breath. He held her as if he was starving for the taste of her, and meant to make up for every minute of every day they'd been apart.

Christy's arms encircled his neck, her

mouth finding his. She kissed him over and over in an agony of need.

With a shudder Cody tore his mouth from hers and spread a wildfire of kisses over her face. His arms were around her waist, and her feet dangled several inches off the ground as his chest heaved with deep breaths.

Weeping for joy, Christy pressed her head against his shoulder, feeling completely at ease for the first time since she'd left Montana. She was in Cody's arms. Nothing could hurt her again.

"It might be a good idea if we went inside," he whispered.

Christy nodded. Slowly he released her, and she slid down.

"How'd you get here?" she asked, searching the parking lot for signs of his Cherokee.

"I flew," he explained as his hand stroked the tumbling curls away from her face. "I couldn't leave things between us the way they were. At least not without talking this out face-to-face. I took three days' vacation, hoping we could put an end to this craziness."

Christy was hoping for the same thing. She took his wrist and pulled him inside her small apartment. She closed the door, then turned to face him, her hands behind her.

From the moment she'd come home, she'd stood alone against what seemed like overwhelming forces. Her mother needed her. James needed her. Everyone wanted a part of her until she felt as if she were being torn in two.

"How . . . how'd you know I was home?" she asked once her mind had cleared enough to process her thoughts.

"I phoned the law firm from the airport. They told me you were out with the flu."

Christy couldn't believe what she was hearing. Cody had phoned her at the office!

"You disapprove?" His eyes narrowed.

"No." But her heart was thumping loudly. It wasn't likely anyone had given his inquiry a second thought. Even if they had, she wouldn't be around to answer their questions.

"But the fact that I talked to someone who knew you *and* James upset you, didn't it?" He started to pace her living room. Four long strides covered the entire length of it. He buried one hand in his back pocket while the other massaged the muscles of his neck. "You're so afraid your precious James is going to find out about me."

"That's not true," she denied vehemently.

Too late, Christy realized she probably was the most pathetic sight he'd ever seen.

Her eyes were red and swollen, and she wasn't even dressed. The five-year-old pajamas she was wearing were as sexy as dishcloths. Not that any of this seemed to bother Cody, who was apparently far more interested in arguing with her than ravishing her.

In her emotionally fragile condition Christy was much too weak to withstand a heated verbal exchange. She'd already heard from Taylor, who knew without a doubt what would be best. Russ, too. But they weren't listening to *her.* It was easy for them to dish out advice when they were a thousand miles from the situation.

She was the one on the front line, the one who'd have to face their parents. She seemed to be the only one who appreciated the long years of hard work that had led James to this point in his career. She couldn't, *wouldn't,* ruin his chances now.

If Cody Franklin expected her to buy their happiness at another's expense, then he didn't really know her at all.

He turned to face her. Boldly she met his eyes, staring down the hot accusation she saw in them.

Suddenly Christy felt his anger start to

dissolve, replaced with doubt and pain. Defeated, he expelled a harsh breath. His shoulders sagged. "Forget I ever mentioned James. I didn't come here to fight about him."

"Why did you come?"

He didn't seem to have an answer, or if he did, he wasn't willing to supply it just yet. He looked away from her and plowed his fingers through his hair. "To talk some sense into you and end this confusion before we both go insane."

How Christy wished it was that simple.

"This isn't as complicated as you're making it," he said. "Either you're serious about loving me or you aren't. It should be a matter of setting the record straight, but —"

"I do love you."

"Then why are you wearing another man's ring?" he demanded. He stalked toward her and pulled her hand from behind her back. He frowned as he found her ring finger bare.

"I've only worn James's diamond once. The night of the engagement party," she said, surprised by how strained her voice sounded. "I took it off the minute I walked in the door and haven't put it on since."

Cody's large, callused hand curled over her fingers as he shut his eyes. The muscles in his jaw clenched. Then, moving slowly, as though hypnotized, he lowered his mouth to hers.

Her lips trembled under his and Christy closed her eyes as hard as she could, wanting to shut out the realities that kept them apart. She longed to block out everything, except the man who was holding her so gently.

"We need to talk," he whispered.

"Isn't 'I love you' enough?" she asked. Although he struggled to hold her at bay, Christy spread nibbling kisses at the curve of his neck. She wanted him so much. . . .

Cody released a ragged sigh and propelled himself away from her. He moved so fast and so unexpectedly that Christy nearly stumbled. Bewildered, she caught herself just in time.

By then Cody had put the full distance of the living room between them. "In case it's slipped your mind, I'd like to remind you that you're an engaged woman."

It seemed she was allowed to forget that when she was in Cody's arms. She blinked back her pain. Throwing this farce of an engagement at her now was cruel and unfair.

"If you flew all those miles to remind me of that, then you made a wasted trip." Humiliation tainted her cheeks and it was all she could do not to cover her face with both hands and turn away from him.

For several minutes neither of them spoke. She sensed that they both needed time to compose themselves. Cody continued pacing, while Christy stood rooted, leaning against the door, requiring its solidity to hold her upright. It was a shock to discover how badly she was trembling.

"I need to ask you to do something," Cody said crisply, as if whatever he was about to say didn't involve him.

"All right."

"Break the engagement to James." His dark eyes cut into her with sharp, unquestioning demand.

"Of course. You know I will as soon as I can —"

"I want you to do it now. Today."

Full of anguish and regret, Christy shut her eyes. This had tormented her from the moment she got home and talked to James. Surely Cody realized she didn't want to stay engaged to another man.

"Christy?"

"I . . . can't break it off. Not yet. You know that. James has been working for three months getting ready for this trial. He was as prepared as any attorney could be, and yet one thing after another has gone wrong for him. I can't add to his troubles by —"

"We have no business seeing each other," Cody interrupted. "We didn't when you were in Montana, and we have even less of an excuse now that you're home."

"But I love you."

Her words fell into an uncomfortable silence. Cody didn't answer for so long that she began to worry. His expression told her nothing.

"Love doesn't make everything right," he said, his eyes darkening with bitterness. "I wish it did, but the way we feel about each other doesn't alter one damn thing. You're promised to another man, and that's all there is to it."

"But . . . Cody —"

"Not only do you have his ring, you've set a wedding date."

"I explained all that," she whispered, feeling utterly defenseless.

"There's something you don't seem to understand," Cody said, frowning heavily. "I'm a man of honor, a man of my word . . ."

She nodded. "I couldn't love you as much as I do without knowing the kind of man you are."

"Then you must realize that I can't continue this. You must know how it makes me feel."

She stared at him, barely able to believe she'd been so stupid and selfish. Cody wasn't being possessive or jealous. It wasn't his pride that was injured or his ego. It was his sense of fairness. A matter of honesty.

He slowly shook his head. "For both our sakes, I wish I could be different. I'd like nothing better than to steal away with you for a few days, hold you, kiss you. More than anything else in this world I want to make love to you, but I can't allow that to happen."

Christy wanted all those things, too.

"The fact that you were committed to James bothered me when you were staying with Russ and Taylor. The fact that you didn't want to break the engagement over the phone wasn't unreasonable and I understood it."

Christy now wished she'd put an end to everything two weeks ago. If she had, her life would be so much simpler.

"It wasn't easy to keep my hands off you then, and it's a lot more difficult now." His voice was tight, and he didn't slacken his stride as he continued to pace. "I can't do this any longer. Either you break it off with James, right now, today, or it's over. I'll fly back to Montana and this will be the last time I see you."

Christy felt as if the entire ceiling had come crashing down on her head.

"The last time?" she repeated, struggling to keep her voice from rising.

"Christy, look at it from my point of view."

"I am. All I'm asking for . . . all I need is for you to be a little more patient. The trial will be over soon."

"I've been more than patient already."

"But it'll only be for a while. I swear to you," she said urgently, "I'll break it off with James at the first opportunity. But I can't do it now."

Once again her words fell into a void and she was left to wonder at his thoughts. "Cody . . . please," she whispered when she couldn't tolerate the silence anymore.

He pivoted sharply. "I know you. You're warm and loving, and you won't do anything that might hurt another person. You refuse to disappoint anyone — except yourself."

If he understood her so well, then surely he'd be patient just a little longer. She was about to say that when he added, "You've allowed your parents to manipulate you all your life."

"That's not true," she burst out, wanting to defend herself, angry that he'd even suggest it.

"They handpicked a husband for you, and you went along with it."

Her shoulders slumped, but her indignation had yet to cool.

"You didn't love James then and you don't love him now. Or so you claim."

"I love *you*," she cried. "How many times do I have to say it?"

"Yet when James offered you an engagement ring, you accepted his proposal."

"I . . . I . . ." Her outrage went limp for lack of an argument. Everything he said was true, but it had happened before she'd met Cody.

"You're so eager to take care of everyone else you're willing to sacrifice your own happiness."

"All I need is a few more days, just until this trial . . ." She didn't finish, since nothing she said was going to change his mind.

"Frankly I have a strong suspicion that you're going to wake up one fine morning married to dear old James and not realize how it happened."

"That's ridiculous." She folded her arms to ward off an unexpected chill. "I swear to you that will never happen."

"You swore to me you were going to break the engagement when you arrived back in Seattle, too. Remember?"

His eyes challenged her to deny it. She couldn't. He met her stare, but it was Christy who looked away first, Christy whose gaze flickered under the force of the truth.

"But how could I have known about the engagement party?" she asked weakly. Then, gaining conviction, she said, "You're not being fair. To even suggest I'd go ahead with the wedding is —" she searched for the right word "— ludicrous."

"Is it really?"

"Of course it is! You make me sound like some weak-willed . . . I can't imagine why you'd want anything to do with me if that's how you feel."

"I love you, Christy, and it's going to hurt like crazy to walk away from you. My request isn't unreasonable, although I know you don't agree with that."

She leaned against the door frame. "You can't ask me to make that kind of decision! Not right this minute. I need time. . . ." In the back of her mind she was desperately praying the Mulligan case would be thrown out of court that afternoon and this whole regrettable affair could be laid to rest.

She might win the lottery, too, but she couldn't count on it.

"Is the decision that difficult?" Cody

asked, frowning. "That on its own says something, whether you admit it or not."

Christy shut her eyes and took a deep breath. The man she loved, her entire future, was about to walk out the door, and she knew of no way to stop him short of destroying another person's happiness.

Straightening, she glared at Cody across the room. "I don't know what's right anymore," she said defiantly. "How can I? All everyone does is make demands of me. First it's Mom and then James and now . . . you."

Then she started to cry. She couldn't help it. Her shoulders shook and her chest heaved as the sobs convulsed her and tears cascaded down her cheeks.

She heard Cody mutter a swear word. "Christy, please, I can't stand to see you cry," he whispered hoarsely.

He could break her heart, but he couldn't stand to see her cry. Christy found the thought almost laughable.

Cody moved across the room and took her in his arms. His hands stroked the hair away from her brow. With him she felt secure. With him she felt warm and protected. She hid her face in his shoulder as the emotion worked through her. He held her until she was able to draw in a deep, shaky breath. Christy could feel her control slipping back into place.

Still Cody held her, his hands caressing her back. For the longest time he said nothing. He continued to hold her close, and after several minutes Christy became aware of how intimate their position was.

She sighed longingly and tested her discovery by tenderly kissing his neck. A moment passed in which she waited for him to protest or ease himself away.

Experiencing a small sense of triumph when he didn't, she leisurely investigated the warm, tantalizing skin, making slow, moist circles over the hollow of his throat.

"Kiss me," she whispered. "Oh, please, Cody, just kiss me. I'll be all right if you do that."

He didn't immediately comply; in fact, he seemed inclined to ignore her, as if nothing would be proved, nothing would be solved by kissing.

He froze when she placed her hands on each side of his strong face, sliding her lips up his jawline and over his chin until their mouths were joined.

Cody pulled his mouth from hers. His whole body seemed to be shaking as he inhaled. He walked over to her sofa and sat on the edge, his elbows on his knees. "What are we going to do?" He shook his head in despair. "I'm not strong enough to walk away from you," he said starkly. "I thought I could."

"I won't let you go." She sat next to him, resting her forehead on his shoulder, and sighed. "I love you so much. . . . I'd give anything to marry you today."

Cody went stock-still. "What did you just say?"

Eleven

"I won't let you go, Cody. I can't," Christy repeated.

"Not that," he said, bolting to his feet. He started pacing again, and when she didn't immediately speak, he added, "It was after that."

She frowned. "I love you?"

"Not that, either. The part about marrying me today."

"I would." She didn't feel any hesitation in saying as much. Almost from the first day she'd met the sheriff of Custer County, she'd known she was going to love him all the days of her life.

"Will you marry me, Christy?" His expression was so open and sincere that she felt tears stinging her eyes.

"Oh, yes," she whispered. She'd probably be the only woman in the world engaged to two men at the same time, but that couldn't be helped.

"I mean now."

"Now?"

"I'd like us to be married this afternoon."

Her heart responded with a quick, wistful beat, but Christy didn't see how a wedding, that day, would be possible.

"Maybe it's different in Montana, but Washington state has a three-day waiting period after we apply for the license."

A satisfied smile lifted the corners of his mouth. "Idaho doesn't."

"That may be, but Idaho's over 350 miles from here. If you're only going to be in Seattle three days, we'll end up spending two of them on the road."

"That's easily fixed. I'll rent a plane." He smiled a breathtaking smile that was so appealing, she thought she'd die a slow death if he didn't make love to her soon. "Am I going too fast for you?"

"No," she rushed to assure him, although her mind was abuzz. "It's just that I'm having trouble understanding. What about James?" She hated mentioning fiancé number one, but she had to be sure they were doing the right thing for the right reasons.

"What about him?"

"Will I . . . do I have to tell him about the wedding? I mean, it won't make much difference if he learns I've married you a couple of days from now or even next week. I'm only suggesting I delay telling him because of the trial."

Some of the happy excitement left Cody's eyes. "I'll leave that up to you. As far as James is concerned, I don't know what's right or wrong anymore. All I know is that I love you more than I thought it was possible to love any woman. It scares me to think I could lose you."

"There isn't the slightest chance of that."

His smile was sad. "I meant what I said earlier about being afraid you'd end up married to James. I've had nightmares about it, wondering if I'd get a call in the middle of the night. I actually dreamed that you phoned to explain how everything got out of your control and you'd married James before you could come up with a way to stop the ceremony."

"I would never allow such a thing."

He gave her a distrusting look, and although it injured her pride to admit it, Christy could understand Cody's concern.

"I feel a whole lot better making *sure* that couldn't happen." The warmth in his eyes removed the sting his words might have inflicted. "I learned a long time ago to cover all my bases. Marrying like this might not be the best thing, but we're making a commitment to each other, and heaven help me for being so weak, but I need that."

Heaven help *him!* Christy felt herself go soft. "Oh, Cody, I love you so much."

"Good," he said, his voice slightly husky, "because you're about to become my wife."

He smiled, completely disarming her. If Christy had a single argument, which she didn't, one of those devastating smiles would have settled it.

"How soon can you be ready?"

"An hour?"

"I'll check the phone book and make the arrangements while you dress." He took her hands and helped her to her feet, pausing long enough to plant a kiss on her unsuspecting lips.

In a daze Christy walked into her bedroom and searched through her closet for something special enough for her wedding. Smiling to herself, she walked to the door and leaned idly against it. "The whole thing's off. I don't have anything decent to wear," she said, teasing him.

Cody sat at her kitchen table, leafing through the impossibly thick yellow pages. He glanced up and chuckled. "Don't worry about it. Whatever you put on is going to come off so fast it'll make your head spin."

Christy chose a soft pink suit she'd purchased the year before at Easter. Carrying it into the bathroom, she closed the door. Quite by accident she caught her reflection in the mirror above the sink and gasped at the pitiful sight she made.

Leaning over the sink, she studied the woman who stared back at her. Her short dark hair was a mess, as if it hadn't been combed in weeks. Her eyes were another thing. Christy had always considered her distinctive blue eyes to be her best feature. Now they were red-rimmed and bloodshot as if she'd been on a two-day drunken spree. Her lips were red and swollen, although she attributed that to Cody's kisses. That man could kiss like nobody's business. She went weak all over again, remembering the feel and taste of his mouth on hers.

Bracing her hands against the sink, she was forced to admit that she was probably among the most pathetic creatures on earth. Yet Cody had looked at her as if she was gorgeous.

The man definitely loved her. That worked out well, since she definitely loved him.

Cody couldn't keep still. He couldn't seem to make himself stop pacing Christy's living room. Four steps, turn, four more steps, turn again.

He glanced at his watch. She was already five minutes past the hour she'd told him she'd need. What could be taking her so long? She'd locked herself in the bathroom, and he hadn't heard a peep since. His mind was beginning to play cruel tricks on him. Perhaps she'd changed her mind about going through with the wedding and, not wanting to hurt his feelings, she'd climbed out the bathroom window.

That thought revealed the shocking state of his mental condition more than anything he'd said or done in the past two hours. He'd flown into Seattle with one purpose. Either he'd settle this craziness between him and Christy or he'd end their relationship.

He hadn't counted on her enthusiasm. She'd been giddy with happiness when he'd arrived. Okay, he was the giddy one. He'd had no idea she was going to throw herself into his arms the moment she opened the door. Not that he'd minded . . . A slow smile relaxed his mouth. Everything had progressed naturally from there.

Cody had always considered himself a strong man. Not muscular or brawny, although he could hold his own and often had. His real strength, he felt, was his stubborn determination. He liked to think he had a will of iron.

Christy had proved him wrong in world-record time.

During the early-morning flight, he'd given himself a pep talk, outlining everything he intended to say. He'd planned to meet with her, explain his position and ask her as calmly and unemotionally as possible to make her decision.

It was either James or him.

If she chose the attorney, Cody was prepared to accept her choice serenely and walk out of her life.

Other than the rocky beginning of that conversation, everything had gone as he'd hoped. Never mind that Christy had managed to break down his resolve within five seconds. The instant she was in his arms, he could feel himself start to weaken.

No woman, not even Becca, had ever had as much control over him.

Now he and Christy would be flying into Coeur d'Alene, Idaho, and getting married. Smiling, Cody settled against the back of the sofa. He recalled when Russ and Taylor had come back to Cougar Point after serving as chaperones for the drill team, traveling with a busload of high school girls to Reno. They'd left town barely speaking to each other and arrived home a few days later married.

Cody could still remember how surprised everyone was. Most folks agreed Taylor was the best thing ever to happen to the opinionated Russ Palmer, but there'd been skeptics, too.

Understandably. Taylor was a city girl. Russ was a rancher. Taylor had only been in town three months.

But when folks in Cougar Point learned that Cody had married Christy after knowing her less than *one* month, there'd be even more raised eyebrows.

That didn't disturb Cody in the least. He loved Christy beyond a doubt, and next month when he stood before the citizens of Custer County to be sworn in as sheriff, she'd be at his side. It would be the proudest moment of his life, and he wanted her with him.

The bathroom door opened, and Christy stepped out. Cody turned around to inform her that she was twelve minutes late. His teasing comment wilted before ever making it to his lips.

She was stunningly beautiful, dressed in a pink linen suit. Her hair was perfect, her makeup flawlessly applied. Christy Manning was so beautiful, Cody couldn't help staring at her. It took more effort than he could believe just to close his mouth. He was too tongue-tied to utter a single word.

"Do I look all right?" she asked, gazing at him expectantly.

For the life of him, all Cody could do was nod.

Christy smiled and held out her hand. "Then let's get this show on the road."

The ceremony itself took place later that evening in a wedding chapel overlooking the crystal blue waters of Lake Coeur d'Alene. Between the time they obtained the license, purchased a pair of gold bands and made the arrangements for the wedding itself, Cody half expected Christy to express some doubts.

She didn't. When she repeated her vows, Christy's strong, clear voice had sounded so confident and poised, he couldn't help marveling — and feeling both humbled and honored by her love.

The flight back to Seattle brought them into the airport shortly before midnight. In the space of one day Cody had traveled from Montana to Washington state, then had flown a two-seater Cessna from Seattle to Coeur d'Alene and back again. He should've been exhausted, but he wasn't. In fact, he felt more alive than he could ever remember being in his life. All he had to do was glance at Christy, who delighted in flashing him a sexy, slightly naughty smile, to feel the blood shoot through his veins.

They returned the Cessna to the hangar and headed toward his rental car. He held the door for her and pressed a light kiss on her lips when she climbed inside. She leaned against him, and it took all his restraint not to deepen the kiss right then and there.

He needed a moment to let his mind clear. "Where to, Mrs. Franklin?" he asked, sliding behind the wheel of the car.

She responded with a blank look.

"Choose any hotel you'd like." He wanted the best Seattle had to offer for Christy. A honeymoon suite. Champagne. Silk sheets. Room service.

"But I didn't pack anything," she protested.

Cody was about to comment that she wouldn't need any clothes, but he didn't get the chance.

"I have this white silk baby doll gown. Would you mind if we went back to my apartment so I could put a few things together?"

"Your wish is my command, Mrs. Franklin."

Resting her head against his shoulder,

Christy sighed audibly and murmured, "I like that in a man."

At the apartment complex, he went inside with Christy. His own suitcase was still there.

Christy hurried into the bedroom, then reappeared a moment later. She walked shyly up to him, then placed her hands on his chest. Cody gazed down at her as she slipped her arms around his neck and kissed him soundly.

Cody's response was immediate. He cradled the back of her head as he returned her kiss — and then some. Soon she was weak and pliant in his arms.

"What was that for?" he asked when he found his breath.

"Because I'm so happy to be your wife."

Cody locked his hands at the small of her back and glanced longingly toward her bedroom.

Christy reached up, kissed his cheek and deftly removed the Stetson from his head. Cody frowned when she tossed it Frisbee fashion across the room. It landed on a chintz-covered cushion as neatly as if he'd set it there himself.

Next her fingers were busy working loose the knot of his tie. "Christy?" Her name tumbled from his lips. "What are you do-ing?"

"Undressing my husband. I've decided I don't want to go to a hotel room, not when we're both here. Not when I can't wait another minute for us to act like a married couple."

"You're sure?" He didn't know why he was questioning her; he wanted her so much that he was trembling.

"Very sure." After discarding his tie, she began to unfasten his shirt buttons.

Cody's hands roved her back, his fingers seeking and not finding a zipper.

She peeled open his shirt and lightly ran her long nails down his bare chest. Shudders swirled down his spine as she nuzzled his neck, nibbling and sucking and licking her way to the throbbing hollow of his throat.

"Christy," he pleaded, his hands on her bottom. "Where's the zipper to your skirt?"

Smiling, she broke away long enough to remove the suit jacket and kick off her heels, which went flying in opposite directions. She twisted around and unfastened the button at her side, then slid the zipper open so the skirt could fall past her hips and pool at her feet. Stepping out of it, she reached behind her for the row of buttons that ran down the back of her silk blouse.

"I can do that," he said eagerly. His fingers fumbled awkwardly with the tiny buttons, but he managed. Her blouse and her lacy bra followed the path of his shirt, landing on the carpet somewhere between the sofa and television.

Unable to wait a second longer, Cody kissed her, his tongue surging into her mouth. The minute she leaned into him, Cody felt his body heat rise to the boiling point.

Slipping her arms around his neck, Christy let her head fall back, grazing his bare chest with her breasts.

He groaned, fighting the rising flames of his passion. She was slowly, surely, driving him out of his mind.

"Christy," he begged, not knowing exactly what he was pleading for. Not for her to stop, that much he knew. *More,* he decided. He needed more of her.

Tucking his arms behind her knees, he lifted her up and carried her into the bedroom. The only light was the soft illumination from the single lamp in the living room.

Gently he placed her on the bed, and they hastily finished undressing each other. Cody looked down on her, nestled in the thick folds of a lavender comforter. She was so beautiful that for a moment he was lost to everything but the woman before him. He longed to tell her what he felt, and knew it would be impossible to put into words.

Lightly he ran his hands over her breasts and smiled. . . .

Afterward he lay on his back with Christy beside him, her head on his shoulder, her arm draped over his chest. Cody sighed as she cuddled her body intimately against his.

Her eyes remained closed, her smile dreamy. "I guess I'm not a good girl anymore."

"Oh, yes, you are. Very good, indeed . . ."

"What are you doing now?" Cody murmured.

He was half asleep, Christy saw as she caught his earlobe between her teeth. "I'm making a citizen's arrest."

"Oh, yeah? What's the charge?"

"I'll trump something up later."

"Christy, hey, what are you wearing?"

"My new silk nightgown."

"I like you better with nothing on."

Ignoring his complaints, she straddled his hips and leaned forward to kiss his chin.

"Mmm, you smell good . . . flowers, I think."

"Remember, you're the one who emptied an entire bottle of bubble bath into my tub."

"You didn't object."

"How could I? You were doing your husbandly duty and pampering me . . . only . . ." She paused and drew in a soft breath as he closed his hands over her breasts. "I didn't realize it could be done in a tub."

"It?" he teased.

"Cody, I was supposed to be the one arresting you, remember?"

"Say it." He raised the silk gown high on her leg and began to caress her thighs with both hands.

"It embarrasses me to say it . . . Cody," she whimpered as his finger executed the sweetest of punishments.

"You *are* going to say it."

She couldn't utter a single word. She hadn't known her body was capable of giving her any more pleasure than it already had.

"I love it when you blush," he murmured.

Christy rested her head on his chest, listening to the steady, even beat of his heart. "Are we ever going to sleep?" she asked.

"Nope. The way I figure it we've got about

forty-eight hours before my plane leaves, and at the rate we're going we can make love —"

"I'm too tired."

Christy felt him smile against her hair. "I am, too." he said. "We'll make up for lost time in the morning."

"In the morning," she echoed as her eyes slowly drifted closed.

A horrible racket woke Christy several hours later. She bolted upright and glanced at her clock radio. Just after 4:00 a.m.

Cody was already out of bed and reaching for his pants.

"Christy?"

The slurred voice belonged to none other than her brother Rich. She'd given him an extra key to her apartment. He stopped in often, but had always phoned first.

"It's my brother. He has a key. Stay here. I'll get rid of him."

"Your brother?"

"Shh." She grabbed her robe, then kissed Cody before hurrying into the living room.

Rich stood by the door, looking like an errant schoolboy. "Hi," he said, raising his right hand.

"I don't suppose you know what time it is?"

"Late," he offered.

"How about early."

"How early?"

"Too early," she told him, praying he wouldn't notice the two sets of clothes spread from one end of the living room to the other. She marched across the room and gripped his elbow, turning him toward the door.

He gave her a hurt look. "You're sending me back into the cold?"

"Yes."

"I didn't drive here. I couldn't," he said. "I know you probably can't tell, but I've had a teeny bit too much to drink."

"I noticed."

"I was hoping you'd make me some coffee, listen to my woes and let me sleep on your couch."

"I have to be at work in a few hours." A slight exaggeration. Besides, when she didn't show up at the office, everyone would assume she was still home with the flu.

"Pamela cheated on me," Rich blurted. "I need some advice and I need it from a woman. Just hear me out, okay?"

Not knowing what else she could do, Christy moved into her kitchen and started making a pot of coffee. Rich pulled out a stool at her kitchen counter and plopped

himself down. "Apparently she's been seeing him all along."

"Who?"

"Pamela."

"No, who's she been seeing?" This conversation was frustrating Christy.

"Hell if I know his name. Some jerk."

"It isn't like you were crazy about her."

"Maybe not, but I always thought she was
crazy about me. What is it with women these
days? Isn't anyone faithful anymore?" he
said plaintively.

"Ah . . ."

Rich squinted into the darkened living
room. "Hey, what's going on here?" Standing, he walked over to the chintz-covered
chair and picked up Cody's Stetson. He
glanced back at his sister.

"I can explain," she said in a weak voice.

Frowning, he returned to the kitchen and
carefully placed the Stetson on her head.
Several sizes too large, it rested well below
her hairline in the middle of her forehead.

"Is there something you wanted to tell
me?" he asked.

TWELVE

"Who the hell are you?" Rich demanded.

Christy shoved the Stetson farther back on her head to find Cody walking out of the bedroom.

"It sounded like you might need a little help explaining things," her husband said casually.

Rich pointed at his sister and his mouth fell open. His eyes had narrowed, and disdain and disbelief marked his handsome features.

"It's not as bad as it looks," Christy said, ignoring his censure. Acting as nonchalant as she could, she poured him a cup of coffee.

Swiveling his gaze between Cody and Christy, Rich shook his head. "It looks pretty darn bad, little sister." He stared at the trail of clothing on the living-room carpet. His mouth twisted with disgust as he started toward the front door. "In fact, I don't think I've got the stomach to listen to you."

"You'll listen to her," Cody warned grimly, striding toward Rich. The two men stood no more than two feet apart, glaring at each other ferociously.

"And who's going to make me? You?" Rich's sarcasm was sharp. "If that's what you think, I've got news for you, cowboy."

"Rich, shut up," Christy said. "The least you can do is hear what I have to say."

"I don't listen to —"

"Don't say it," Cody interrupted, his words so cold they almost froze in midair. "Because if you do, you'll live to regret it."

Rich mocked him with a smile. "Listen, Mr. Marlboro Man, I've taken about enough from —"

"Stop it, both of you!" Christy marched out from her kitchen. She stood between her husband and her brother, a hand on each man's chest, and glanced up at Rich. "I'd like to introduce you to my husband, Cody Franklin. Cody, this stupid oaf is my third-youngest brother, Rich."

"Your husband!"

"My husband," she echoed softly. She dropped her hands and slipped her arm around Cody's waist, leaning against him, needing his solid strength.

"I'll have you know," Cody muttered, "you interrupted my wedding night."

"Your husband," Rich repeated a second time, stalking across the room. He retrieved Christy's bra from the floor and twirled it around on one finger. "I don't suppose James knows about this?"

Christy snatched her underwear out of her brother's hand. "As a matter of fact, he doesn't."

"This is getting even more interesting." Sitting on the sofa, he picked up Cody's shirt and made a soft tsking sound with his tongue. "What about Mom and Dad?"

"They don't know, either," Cody said forcefully.

"Aha," Rich snickered, "the plot thickens."

"I'm so pleased you find this amusing." Christy moved hastily about the room, picking up pieces of discarded clothing, more embarrassed than she could ever remember being.

Cody poured himself a cup of coffee and joined Rich, sitting on the opposite end of the sofa. "I'm a good friend of Russ Palmer's," he said by way of explanation.

Rich nodded. "So my dear, sweet sister met you when she was in Montana visiting Taylor?"

"Cody's the one who drove her to the

hospital," Christy added. She sat on the side of the sofa and curved her arm around Cody's broad shoulders.

"Then this was what you'd call a whirlwind courtship." Rich studied the two of them. "Exactly how long have you known each other?"

"Long enough," Cody answered, making it plain he didn't much care for this line of questioning.

"We didn't mean to fall in love so fast," Christy continued, wanting to untangle any doubts Rich had about her relationship with Cody. "It just happened."

"You might have mentioned it to James."

"I probably should've phoned and told him while I was still in Montana, but it seemed wrong to break the engagement over the phone, and then when I got home —"

"The surprise engagement party," Rich said, groaning loudly. "I can see that you were trapped. Mom put her heart and soul into that party. You couldn't back out without humiliating her. Not at the last minute like that."

"I wanted to tell James right away, but that didn't work out, either." The hopelessness of the entire situation nearly overwhelmed her. "The Mulligan trial was called early, and he's immersed himself in the most complicated case of his career. He's got to be emotionally and physically at his peak for that."

"Yeah, that's right," Rich commented. "I'd forgotten about that."

"The timing couldn't be worse. I can't tell James about Cody and me until he's through with the trial. And yet . . ."

Rich released a long, sympathetic sigh. "You do seem to have your problems, little sister."

Cody leaned against the back of the sofa. "You can imagine how I felt when I learned she'd been roped into that engagement party. To complicate matters, she set a date for the wedding."

Rich did a pitiful job of disguising a smile. "November 12, wasn't it?"

"That's not funny, Rich, so cut the comedy, will you?" Christy playfully punched his upper arm.

"You have to admit, it's kind of amusing."

Christy found very little of this amusing. She was deliriously pleased to be Cody's wife, but he was flying out of Seattle in another day, and she'd have to return to her job and live a complete lie with James and her parents. She wouldn't be able to keep up this charade for long.

"Perhaps this predicament is comical to

someone else," Cody said grudgingly, "but trust me, it isn't if you're one of the parties involved."

Rich was quick to agree. "So the two of you decided to take matters into your own hands and get married."

Christy nodded. Her eyes met Cody's, and they exchanged a loving look. His fingers linked with hers. "It must sound crazy."

"Hey, it works for me," Rich said, "but I wouldn't be in your shoes for all the tea in China when you tell Mom and Dad what you did."

"Why not?" Cody asked with a dark frown.

"They were cheated out of one wedding when Taylor married Russ without a single family member present. I can only speculate what they'll say when they hear Christy did the same thing."

"They'll skin me alive," she muttered. In all the excitement, in all her enthusiasm, Christy had forgotten how much her mother was looking forward to planning her wedding — which would be far more elaborate than the engagement party. As they left the Eagles Hall that dreadful night, Elizabeth Manning had been filled with ideas and opinions and excitement.

"Your parents won't do any such thing," Cody insisted.

"Cody, you don't know them." Christy felt a return of the nausea that had overtaken her at the party. Elizabeth Manning might never forgive her, and she'd always done what her mother thought best. Until now.

"They won't say a word," he said softly, "because I won't let them."

"But you don't understand —"

"If your parents are looking for someone to blame, they can deal with me. I was the one who insisted you marry me now. You just went along with it."

"Because I'm crazy in love with you and because I want to be your wife more than I've ever wanted anything."

"Hey," Rich said, raising both hands, "if both of you want to stand in front of the firing squad, I'm not going to stop you."

A chill descended on the room. "I take it there was a reason for this unexpected visit," Cody said pointedly.

"I was having woman problems," Rich mumbled.

"I thought there was something bothering you the night of the party." Although Rich hadn't enlightened her with the details, Christy should've known something was amiss. Otherwise he would have noticed how upset she was that evening.

"I may be having a few problems," Rich

continued. "But they're nothing compared to what you two are facing. Married to one man while engaged to another — that, little sister, takes the cake."

"How kind of you to point it out." Yawning, she covered her mouth with her hand. "I'll make you a bed on the sofa and you can spend the rest of the night there."

"And interrupt your honeymoon?"

"It's already been interrupted," Cody reminded him. "If there's any justice in this world, I'll be able to return the favor someday."

"No chance of that. I'm swearing off women. The whole lot of them," Rich said with an emphatic shake of his head.

"Oh?" Christy had heard that song before.

"It's true. They're fickle, money-hungry, materialistic —"

"Thank you very much," Christy said, standing.

"With a few exceptions." He eyed his sister and smiled in apology.

"Now where was it you said you wanted to go for dinner?" Cody asked, reaching for his suit jacket.

"What's the matter with eating here?" Christy asked, not wanting to leave the apartment. Everything had been idyllic, and she was almost light-headed with happiness. To walk outside these protected walls might well invite trouble, and she'd had enough of that to last her a lifetime.

"I thought you wanted to dine out?"

"Not really." At the time he'd made the suggestion, Christy hadn't been able to think of an excuse. Now her mind overflowed with them, only she doubted Cody would consider any of them sensible.

She checked her freezer and extracted a package of pork chops. "I could wrestle us up some grub in no time." She turned around and grinned. "Am I beginning to sound like a Montana woman?"

"No. You're beginning to sound like a cattle thief." He moved behind her, slid his arms around her waist and nuzzled the curve of her neck.

"I'm a good cook."

"I know."

"How could you? Every time I go to make something for us, you interrupt me with . . . you know."

"Are you still having trouble saying the words?"

"No . . ." She giggled softly. "You've cured me of that." Twisting around, she leaned against the refrigerator door with her hands primly linked in front of her. "I can talk about making love about as often as you want to do it."

"Then let's get out of here before you give me any ideas."

"I like giving you ideas."

Cody glanced at his watch. "It's well past dinnertime and I'm hungry."

She moistened her lips. "You want me to say some of the other words you taught me?"

"Christy . . . no."

"Come here." She beckoned him with her index finger. "I'll whisper a couple of humdingers in your ear."

Cody ignored her. "I'm not going to let you sidetrack me."

"Oh, but I enjoy sidetracking you."

"That's the problem," Cody said. "I like it, too." He cleared his throat and changing tactics, grabbed his hat. "As your husband, I command that we leave for dinner now."

"You command?" She couldn't help laughing.

"That's right," he said, his mouth quivering with a suppressed smile. "I've got to teach you that I'm wearing the pants in this family."

"If that's the case, then why are they so often unzipped?"

Cody actually blushed, and Christy smiled.

"Because I'm a needy husband," he said gruffly. "Are you complaining?"

"Oh, no." She sent him a saucy grin. "Because I happen to be a needy wife. In fact, I seem to be experiencing a need right now. Is it hot in here to you?"

"Christy?" Cody's voice contained a low note of warning.

"It seems very hot . . . much too hot for all these clothes." She jerked the light sweater over her head and let it fall to the floor. Next she lowered the straps of her bra. "There," she said with a deep sigh, offering Cody what she hoped was a tantalizing display of her assets. "That feels better."

Cody stood his ground for a couple of minutes. Then he removed his hat and sent it flying across the room.

Silently Christy rejoiced.

"What about those jeans? Aren't they making you hot, too?" Cody asked.

"Maybe they are. Only I can't seem to open the snap." He didn't seem to notice that she hadn't tried.

"I see." He stepped over to her and made short work of her bra, then cupped Christy's breasts, his hands firm and insistent.

Sighing, Christy closed her eyes, giving

herself over to a host of delightful sensations. Cody used one hand to stroke her breast, his other hand busy at the opening of her jeans. The zipper purred, and Christy was filled with another small sense of triumph.

She shivered helplessly as Cody slid her jeans down her hips. Her bikini underwear followed and that was the last thing she noticed for some time. Other than Cody, of course . . .

Christy's gaze fell reluctantly on Cody's luggage, which lay open on her bed. The lump in her throat seemed to grow larger every minute, until she could hardly swallow. She'd decided earlier that she wasn't going to be emotional when he left. They'd talked everything out earlier, planned for their future as best they could.

"You called the office?" Cody asked, putting a clean shirt in the suitcase.

"Yes . . . I told them I still had the flu." Lying didn't come easy to Christy. She felt as though she'd dug herself into a deep pit.

"What did they say?"

"Marcia, she's the office manager, said it's a slow week and not to worry about it, but she did make a point of asking me if I'd be in on Friday, which seemed a little odd."

"What about James?"

"He was at the courthouse." Her eyes widened at the unexpectedness of the question.

"When's the last time you heard from him?"

"Ah . . ." She had to stop and think. "The day after the engagement party. We talked briefly, and he explained that he wouldn't be able to keep in touch while the trial's going on." Under normal circumstances she would've seen him at the office, even if it was only for a few minutes, every morning. The fact that he hadn't made an effort to contact her said a good deal about their relationship.

"I see." Cody was obviously surprised.

"He's very intense and single-minded."

"Do you think he'll get an acquittal?"

"I don't know," she said.

"Whatever happens, this can't go on much longer. You realize that, don't you?"

"It won't be more than a few days." In discussing the situation they'd agreed on a time limit. Even if the trial dragged on for more than a week, Christy had promised to return James's ring and tell her parents that she and Cody were married.

"I still think we should tell your parents now."

"Not yet," she pleaded. The way Christy figured it, she'd start dropping hints so the fact that she'd married Cody wouldn't come as such a shock. After Cody flew back to Montana, she intended to drop by the family home and casually point out that James hadn't called her once since the party. She was hoping her parents would conclude that perhaps he wouldn't be the best husband for her, after all.

"Christy, I'm worried." Cody stood in front of her, his face concerned. "I don't like leaving you, especially under these circumstances."

"You know I love you."

His mouth curved into a sensual smile. "Beyond a doubt."

"Good." She put her arms around his waist and hugged him close. His heart beat strongly and evenly, offering her reassurance. In time they'd look back on these bleak days and laugh, she told herself. Someday, but not now.

"I'll phone you twice a day," he promised in a husky whisper. "Morning and night."

"I'll need that."

"So will I."

A sigh of regret rumbled through his chest as he dropped his arms. "It's time to go."

Neither of them seemed inclined to talk

on the ride to the airport. Once Cody had checked in at the airline counter, he hugged Christy and kissed her lightly. It was as if he dared not kiss her the way they both enjoyed for fear he wouldn't be able to walk away. She understood all too well.

"Take care of yourself," she whispered.

"You, too."

She nodded, barely conscious of the way she clung to him. "Of course. We'll talk tonight. And before we know it, we'll be together."

"Together for good," he added. "I've got to go."

She closed her eyes tightly to keep from crying.

Cody kissed her again, only this time his mouth was fierce and wild. He released her by degrees, his reluctance tearing at her heart. With everything in her, Christy longed to board the plane with him. How much easier it would be to leave with Cody and then call James and her parents. But Christy knew she couldn't abandon her responsibilities. Cody understood that, too; she was sure of it. Christy Manning Franklin had always done the right thing, even if it was sometimes for the wrong reasons.

The next morning Christy returned to work

for the first time since she'd left for vacation. What a difference a few weeks could make. She wasn't the same woman anymore.

"Christy." James's voice rose as he hurried over to her desk. "You're back. I hope you're feeling better."

For all his brilliance, James had very little experience of life. That was even more obvious to Christy now, and it made her feel oddly protective of him. She smiled as he reached for her hand, squeezing her fingers. Kissing her, even in an empty office, would have been unthinkable. He'd never been openly affectionate, but he was tender and good, and Christy couldn't ignore her guilty conscience.

"I'm much better, thanks. How's the Mulligan case going?"

He frowned and briefly looked away before responding. "Not too well."

"How much longer do you think it's going to be?"

"I'm hoping to wrap everything up by the end of next week."

"That long?" She couldn't keep the disappointment out of her voice.

James frowned again. "I didn't realize how negatively this case was affecting you."

"It's just that . . ." She couldn't very well

announce that she was looking for the right moment to tell him she was married to someone else.

"I know, darling." He said the last word softly, as though fearing someone might overhear him. "This is a difficult time for us both, but it'll soon be over, and we can get on with our lives."

Now that Christy had a chance to study him, she saw that he seemed exhausted. Deep lines were etched around his eyes and mouth. Clearly James wasn't sleeping well.

"The case is going worse than you expected, isn't it?"

James sighed. "It's difficult to hide something like this from the one you love. Yes, it's going much worse."

"Is there anything I can do?" Christy found herself asking.

"Nothing," he said, giving her a rare smile. "But your concern is greatly appreciated." He looked at his watch. "It's time I left for the courthouse. I won't be back for the rest of the day."

Christy nodded.

"I suppose we should meet for dinner. After all, it's been a long time since we've gone out. But —"

"Don't worry," Christy interrupted. "I understand." If she was having trouble dealing with a short conversation as James was walking out the door, an entire evening in each other's company would've been unbearable.

"Have a good day," he said gently.

"You, too."

He nodded, but his expression was somber. It was all too apparent that he didn't think he'd be having anything resembling a satisfactory day.

At lunchtime Christy looked up to find Marcia standing at her desk. The office manager had been with the firm for over fifteen years and was one of the finest women Christy knew.

Christy smiled. "Do you need something, Marcia?" After a three-week absence, her desk was piled high with folders.

"Can you come into one of the conference rooms for a minute?"

"Sure."

Leading the way, Marcia paused in front of the wide oak doors and grinned sheepishly. "It's good to have you back from vacation, Christy. It made all of us appreciate how much your bright smile adds to our day." With that she opened the door.

Christy was greeted with a chorus of "Surprise" from her fellow workers. A large cake sat in the center of the table, surrounded by several gaily wrapped packages. She must have looked stunned, because Marcia placed one hand on her shoulder and explained. "It's a wedding shower for you and James."

THIRTEEN

A week had passed since Cody had come back to Cougar Point. By far the longest week of his life. He wanted Christy with him, hungered for her smile and the way her eyes darkened when she looked up at him in that suggestive way.

He loved Christy, and marrying her had helped him cope with the ridiculous set of circumstances in which they found themselves trapped.

He wasn't pleased that she was still engaged to James, but there seemed little he could do about it. If it had been up to him, he'd have settled it before flying out of Seattle, but Christy had been adamant that she was doing the right thing in waiting. Cody wasn't convinced, but the decision had been hers, and he didn't feel he could go against Christy's wishes.

So they were husband and wife. Cody *felt* married. It was as if he'd lived his entire life waiting for this woman. In the too-brief days they'd been together, Cody knew he'd changed. His life's purpose had been focused on his career, and in many ways it still was. Christy, however, added a new dimension to his personality.

She'd taught him to dream.

Unlike Russ, who'd always planned on marriage, Cody had given up hope of ever finding the right woman. It hadn't been a conscious decision; in fact, he wasn't fully aware of it until he met Christy.

He was getting downright philosophical, he mused. Christy gave his life a deeper meaning, and their marriage made everything else more . . . important, somehow.

Someone brighter than he was would have guessed what was happening the first time they'd kissed. He still recalled feeling lost and bewildered. When he learned she was engaged to marry James, Cody had been even more shaken than he dared to admit.

James. The other man's name brought a grim frown. Reluctantly Christy had shown him a picture of the attorney. He looked clean-cut, professional, intelligent. But he guessed that James Wilkens lacked passion. It was difficult to imagine James allowing a little thing like falling in love to overcome his inhibitions.

Throwing off his anxiety about Christy's engagement, he stood, moved into his kitchen and poured a cup of coffee. He was supposed to be packing, getting ready for his move to Miles City, but because of everything that had happened between Christy and him, he'd delayed until the last minute.

Almost everything in the living room was inside cardboard boxes, and Cody headed absently toward the bedroom, intent on getting as much accomplished that evening as he could.

He recognized his mistake immediately.

Christy had never slept on his bed, never even been in this room, but the fires she sparked to life within Cody were more evident there than anywhere else.

Feeling helpless, missing her so much, Cody sat on the end of the bed. He'd married himself one little hellcat. A smile tempted his mouth. She was a seductress in bed, and an angel out of it.

His need for her was insatiable. Half the time they were so impatient for each other that they hadn't bothered to use any birth control. They'd discussed that; if she were to get pregnant, Cody wouldn't mind. In many ways it would please him tremendously, although he admitted the timing would be all wrong for her. Christy had enough pressures on her already.

A week. They'd been apart for seven days, and it felt like an eternity. Dammit all, he wanted her with him.

Now. Not two days from now.

Not next week. *Now.*

His patience was wearing paper-thin. He picked up the phone and called the number he knew by heart. Christy answered on the second ring.

Her voice softened when she heard his. "Soon," she promised in a seductive whisper that nearly drove him crazy.

"How soon?" he demanded.

"A couple more days."

"Forgive me for saying this, but didn't you claim it would be 'a couple of days' a couple of days ago?" His voice was sharp despite his best efforts.

"Yes, but there are complications."

"Aren't there always?"

"Cody, please, don't be angry with me . . ."

"I called because I love you."

"I love you, too," she said, sounding a little bewildered. Cody realized he'd probably pushed too hard and backed off, spending the next few minutes telling his wife he loved her.

When he replaced the receiver, he was

more frustrated than ever.

Cody was enjoying breakfast in the bowling alley early the following morning when Russ showed up. It wasn't unusual for Russ to eat in town, but rarer since he'd married Taylor.

The rancher slid into the booth across from Cody. "I thought I'd find you here."

"You looking for me?" he asked.

"You could say that." Russ turned over the ceramic mug and waited until the waitress came by and filled it for him. He reached for the menu. "You look like hell."

"Nice of you to say so," Cody muttered.

"I didn't come here to pick a fight."

Their friendship was too good for this kind of bickering. "I haven't been sleeping well," Cody admitted reluctantly, sipping his own coffee. Truth be known, he hadn't had a decent night's sleep since he'd flown home from Seattle.

"How's Christy holding up?"

"A lot better than I am." She always managed to sound cheerful, as if it was perfectly normal for a couple to be married three days and then separated for weeks.

"You sure about that?"

Russ's question caught Cody off guard. He narrowed his eyes, wondering if Russ knew something he didn't. Russ's attention seemed to be on the menu.

"I'm not sure of anything," Cody answered thoughtfully. "What makes you ask?"

Typically Russ shrugged. "Nothing in particular." He set aside the menu, declined to order breakfast when Mary delivered Cody's and sat there looking superior. "Go ahead and eat," he said, motioning toward the plate of sliced ham, eggs, hash browns and toast.

"I wasn't planning on letting my meal get cold," Cody informed him frostily. His nerves were shot, and the last thing he needed was his best friend dropping obscure hints.

Cupping the mug with both hands, Russ leaned back in the booth. "Who else knows you and Christy are married?" he asked after a moment.

"Everyone except James and her parents." Christy's three older brothers were all aware of the fact that they'd eloped. Cody had spoken to the two oldest brothers, Paul and Jason, before he'd left Seattle. Rich had been the first to discover their secret, of course, and he'd quickly let the others in on it.

"Should I thank you for the fact that Mrs. Simmons stopped me in the street yesterday with a jar of her watermelon pickles?" Cody asked, eyeing Russ. "She says she heard the sheriff had taken himself a wife and wanted to give me a small gift."

"Ah . . . I might've mentioned something to Mrs. Simmons," Russ said, hiding a smile. Mrs. Simmons handed out home-made preserves at every opportunity. Each family in town ended up with at least one jar every year.

Russ took another drink of his coffee. "I guess you and everyone else in town figured out Taylor got pregnant on our honey-moon."

Cody was having trouble following this conversation. "What's that got to do with anything?"

"Nothing," he said with an enigmatic smile.

"Listen, Russ, if you know something I don't, spit it out, would you? I'm in no mood for games. Is something going on with Christy that I don't know?"

"Did she tell you about the wedding shower?"

Cody scowled. "No. When was this?"

"Last week. The girls in the office held it for her, threw it as a surprise."

"That was nice."

"It wasn't for you and Christy," Russ

barked. "What's with you, man? The shower was for Christy and James."

Cody rubbed his face. She hadn't said a word, not a single word about any wedding shower. And now that he knew, Cody thought that, maybe, just maybe, Christy did sound a little less cheerful than usual. He was fast losing his perspective.

"I bet she hasn't told you something else, either."

Cody resented having his brother-in-law tell him things Christy hadn't even mentioned. "You mean there's more?" he asked darkly. "Did her mother take her shopping and spring for a five-thousand-dollar wedding dress?"

"Nothing quite so drastic," Russ said with a hint of a smile. "I overheard Taylor on the phone last night. She was talking to Christy."

"What did Christy say?"

"I don't know. I only heard half the conversation."

Cody had talked to Christy, too. He'd hung up with a restless feeling he couldn't identify, but he'd attributed it to the fact that she was still in Seattle when he wanted her in Montana.

"And?"

"And when I asked Taylor, she seemed

reluctant to say much. But I heard her discuss symptoms."

"Symptoms?"

"I tried to tell you earlier," Russ informed him with a look that questioned Cody's intelligence, "but you got so damn defensive, I shut up." Russ shook his head. "Taylor got pregnant in Reno. Think about it, Cody. Taylor and Christy are two of *five* children. Doesn't it seem obvious to you that the Manning women are a fertile lot?"

"Christy's not pregnant," Cody said with a confidence he wasn't feeling. He felt his head start to spin.

"You're sure of that?"

"She'd say something if she even suspected. I'd bet on it."

"Of course. She tells you everything."

"I'd like to think she'd confide in me," Cody said, growing more uncertain.

"If she didn't tell you about the wedding shower, you can damn well wager she wouldn't mention that she's hanging her head over a toilet every morning."

Cody felt as if he'd been kicked in the stomach. Christy was pregnant and too concerned about protecting her parents and James to risk telling him.

Hell, she *couldn't* tell him. He hadn't made it easy for her, had he? Missing her the way he did, Cody was irritable and impatient while Christy carried the brunt of the load.

Hastily he slid out of the booth and put on his hat. He'd been looking for an excuse to put an end to this nonsense, and now he had one.

"Where you going?" Russ demanded, reaching across the table for Cody's untouched breakfast plate. He leaned forward and retrieved the salt and pepper shakers.

"Seattle."

Chuckling, Russ nodded. "That's what I thought."

"Enjoy your breakfast," Cody muttered sarcastically.

"Thanks," he responded between bites, "I will."

Christy had been feeling blue all day. Cody wasn't home when she'd tried to call, and that depressed her even more. Nothing made sense. Nothing. She felt weepy and excited. Confused and elated. Engaged to one man. Married to another. She might be pregnant. It might be the beginning of an ulcer. She didn't know which.

She couldn't sleep, although she desperately needed to.

Her appetite was nil. After going through the bother of fixing herself spaghetti and a salad for dinner, her meal sat uneaten on her kitchen table.

Feeling wretched, she sank down in front of the television and turned on the movie channel, silently chastising herself for not writing thank-you notes to her friends from the office. Sending notes of appreciation for gifts she intended to return seemed a ridiculous thing to do.

A 1940s war movie with an incredibly young John Wayne and Maureen O'Hara was on, and she was soon caught up in the fast-paced action. How minor her troubles seemed compared to those on the screen.

Damp tissues crowded her end table. She was sniffling ingloriously when her doorbell chimed.

Whoever was on the other side was certainly impatient. The doorbell rang a second time before she was halfway across the carpet. "Hold your horses," she said peevishly. She wasn't interested in company.

Christy quickly changed her mind.

"Cody," she whispered when she saw her husband. "Oh, Cody." Without another word she broke into tears and flew into his arms.

Seconds later, his mouth was on hers in that urgent, hungry way that was so familiar between them. Cody directed her into the living room, then closed the door with his foot, all the while kissing her.

Christy's hands roamed his face when he released her. She giggled and locked her arms around his neck, holding on to him for everything she was worth.

"Oh . . . Christy, I missed you," he breathed. His hands caressed her face. Then he was kissing her again and again as if he'd never get enough of the taste of her.

"I've been so miserable without you," Christy admitted, feeling weepy and jubilant at the same time.

"Me, too, love." He looked at her for a long moment, frowning, then smiling, then frowning again.

"What is it?" Christy asked, reacting to his confusion but not understanding it. She sensed a wonder in him, too, as if he couldn't quite believe they were married.

Christy believed it. Their love was the only thing that had gotten her through the trauma of the past week.

"Are you pregnant?" he asked without preamble, running his splayed fingers through her hair. His hold on her tightened, but Christy doubted he was aware of it.

Involuntarily her eyes widened at his question. "I . . . I don't know yet."

"You've been ill?"

"Yes . . . How'd you know that?" Usually she'd been sick in the mornings, but often in the afternoons, too. If she was looking for a pattern, there wasn't one. She was confused and anxious, and not knowing where to turn, she'd called her sister. "Taylor?" Christy had never dreamed that her older sister would say anything to Cody. She'd counted on Taylor to be discreet.

"No," Cody admitted, scowling. "I had breakfast with Russ this morning. Rather Russ ate *my* breakfast while he cheerfully pointed out that Taylor got pregnant while they were still in Reno and —"

Christy interrupted him. "You came because of that?"

"No." Cody dropped his hands and stepped away. "Well, not completely. I did come in part because I was afraid . . . no, afraid's the wrong word. I was concerned for you. I came for another reason, too."

He was so sincere, so forthright. "Yes?"

His eyes darkened. "You didn't tell me about the wedding shower."

Christy's gaze fell. "I couldn't."

"I realize that now, and I realize a whole lot more. This has to be the end of it, Christy." His eyes burned into hers. "As your husband — the man that loves you —

I can't let you continue this charade any longer."

Spontaneous tears filled her eyes as she nodded. "I don't think I can pull it off another day. I . . . thought I was doing what was best for everyone involved, but I see now that I was only prolonging the agony — mostly my own. You were right, so right. There'll never be a good time to tell Mom and Dad. I did us both a terrible disservice by refusing to acknowledge that."

Cody's lips brushed her forehead. "Don't be so hard on yourself."

"There's no one else to blame. It's just that it's really difficult for me to disappoint my parents. I love them both so much, and they're so fond of James."

"But they don't have the right to pick your husband for you."

"I know." She exhaled softly. "I would've liked to have spared James this, but he has to know. I . . . I did him a disservice by not telling him the afternoon I came home. James isn't as emotionally fragile as I've made him out to be."

Cody's eyes flared briefly before he spoke. "How soon can we get you in to see a doctor?"

"A doctor?" she asked. "Why?" Sure, she'd been overprotective of James and reluctant about telling her parents the truth, but that didn't mean she needed medical help.

"If you're pregnant —"

"Oh, that," she said, relieved. "Taylor recommended I buy one of those home pregnancy test kits, which I did this afternoon. Only I decided I could deal with *not* knowing better than I could handle knowing. Does that sound crazy?"

Cody chuckled. "No. But do you mind satisfying my curiosity? I, for one, am anxious to find out if I'm going to become a father."

"You definitely are," she said, loving the way Cody's face brightened at her words. "The only question is whether or not it's going to be nine months from now."

Cody's arms were around her, his eyes filled with a tenderness that made her knees grow weak. "The test takes about twenty minutes," she said, sliding her hands up the front of his shirt.

"Twenty minutes," Cody repeated.

She moistened her lips, thrilled when her husband's narrowed gaze followed the seductive movement of her tongue.

"Are you suggesting what I think you're suggesting?" he whispered.

Christy nodded.

"But if you're pregnant, will it hurt the baby?" His voice was hoarse, and a dark flame seemed to leap to life in his eyes.

"Not according to Taylor."

"You're sure?"

"Positive. Besides, it'll do this baby's mother a whole lot of good."

Christy lay contentedly in his arms, her long, sleek body nestled intimately with his. If they spent the next ten years exactly like this, Cody wouldn't have a single complaint. He loved this woman. He loved everything about her.

"Are you disappointed?" she asked softly, rolling over so she could look at him when he answered.

He kissed her, his mouth clinging to hers, his hands caressing her. "You've got to be kidding."

They'd been on fire for each other from the moment he'd arrived. Their hands had trembled as they'd hurriedly undressed each other, their mouths eager, filled with promises and pleas.

Raising herself on one elbow, Christy smiled dreamily down on him and lovingly traced her fingers over the hard angles of his face as though memorizing every feature. To Cody's way of thinking, that was unnecessary. He never planned to leave her again.

"I wasn't talking about the lovemaking," she said. "I was referring to the pregnancy test."

His arm curved around her trim waist. "No. When the time's right, we'll start our family and not because we were in too much of a hurry to —"

"May I remind you how much of a hurry we were in a few minutes ago?"

"No, you may not." He clasped her around the waist and they both dissolved into laughter.

A woman he could love *and* laugh with — how did he get so lucky?

"It might be a good idea if I went over to my parents' house alone," Christy said. She looked up at him beseechingly. "Please, Cody?"

"I won't hear of it, Christy," he answered in a voice that brooked no dissent. "We're in this together."

"But . . ."

"You phoned James?"

"You know I did. He'll arrive at my parents' within the hour." James had sounded surprised to hear from her, and even more perplexed when she explained she needed to speak with him urgently. He'd offered to come to her apartment, but when she'd suggested they meet at her family home in an hour, he'd agreed.

"How did Rich find out we're telling your parents?" Cody asked, frowning.

Her scoundrel of a brother had been visiting their parents when Christy called and in fact had answered the phone. There must have been something in her voice that conveyed her intent, because Rich had made it clear he planned to stay around for the fireworks display. That comment reminded Christy that the coming scene was bound to evoke plenty of emotion. Christy wished Cody would wait for the worst to pass before he presented himself as their latest son-in-law.

"Don't even think of arguing with me," he said. "We're doing this together."

"All right," she murmured, holding in a sigh. "The way I figure it, we'll have forty-five minutes to explain everything to my parents before James arrives."

"Good." Cody nodded.

"Are you ready?" she asked, and her voice trembled despite every effort to maintain an optimistic facade. Her heart felt frozen with fear. Although she'd wanted to handle this on her own, she was grateful Cody had chosen to go with her.

They spoke infrequently on the drive to her parents' home. When they did, it was to murmur words of encouragement, or reinforce how much they loved each other.

As they pulled in to the driveway, another car came in after them. "Oh, no," Christy breathed.

"What's wrong?"

"It's James." Christy climbed out of the car, not waiting for Cody. She turned to face her fiancé. "You're early," she said, struggling to keep the annoyance out of her voice.

"I called your parents, and they suggested I come now." James's gaze narrowed as Cody came to stand behind her and rested his hand on her shoulder.

It was clear that James took offense at the familiar way Cody touched her. His eyes went cold as he demanded, "Who is this?"

FOURTEEN

Christy felt Cody's hand tighten involuntarily. The two men glared at each other like hostile dogs who'd inadvertently strayed into each other's territory. She supposed it wasn't a complimentary analogy, but it seemed fitting.

"James, this is Cody Franklin," she said, hating the unexpected way her voice squeaked.

"So the gang's all here," Rich shouted, coming out the front door, ready to greet the two men. "I suppose you're wondering why I've called this meeting." He laughed, obviously in a playful mood.

Christy glared at him, wondering what he was doing.

"Do you mind waiting a few minutes?" Rich asked. "Jason and Paul are on their way."

"As a matter of fact, I do mind," Christy snapped. She gripped Rich hard by the elbow and forced him back into the house. "Please introduce Cody to Mom and Dad," she said.

Rich's mouth fell open. "Me? No way, little sister. I happen to value my neck."

"I'll take care of everything," Cody said, slapping Rich on the back. "You have nothing to fear but fear itself."

"James," Christy said reproachfully, turning to face the attorney, "it would have helped matters if you'd come when I suggested, but since you're here now, we'll settle this in the kitchen."

She walked into the house and passed her mother, who was watching her curiously.

"We'll talk in the kitchen," Christy reminded James when he hesitated in front of Elizabeth Manning and shrugged.

"Christy?" her father called. "What's going on here?"

"I'll explain everything in a few minutes, but first I have to clear something up with James."

"Actually, I'll be more than happy to explain," Cody said, stepping forward. He offered Eric Manning his hand, and they exchanged a brief handshake as Cody introduced himself.

"Exactly what's going on?" James wanted to know as they entered the kitchen.

Christy stopped at the huge round oak table. She pulled out a chair and sat down, then gestured for James to do the same.

He complied, but with some hesitation. "You never answered my question. Who is that man?"

"Cody Franklin."

"That doesn't explain much."

"No, it doesn't," she agreed readily. With a sigh, she wondered where she should even begin. "He's from Montana."

"Ah, that accounts for the cowboy hat."

"We met when I went to spend time with Taylor. Cody's the new sheriff of Custer County."

James nodded, urging her to go on. She'd explained the easy part; everything else was hard.

Unable to stay seated, Christy surged to her feet and frowned as she organized her thoughts. "Sometimes, not often I think, but sometimes when two strangers meet something happens . . . something special." She paused and looked at James, hoping, praying she'd see a glimmer of understanding. She didn't.

"You're talking about fairy tales," he said, and laughed as though she'd made a poor joke. "Are you going to break into song next?"

Christy ignored the question. "A special magic, a chemistry that flows between the two of them," she went on. "There was magic when Taylor met Russ. At first they both resisted it and —"

"Yes, yes," James interrupted, "but what have your sister and her husband got to do with anything?"

"Cody and I experienced that same . . . chemistry," she announced, astonished this genius attorney could be so obtuse. "Neither of us was expecting to fall in love."

"You didn't," James said flatly, dismissing her claim.

"But I did."

"You can't be in love with Franklin. It isn't possible when you're in love with me."

"James, please, let me explain —"

He interrupted with an upraised hand. "Christy, darling, what you experienced for this man is a simple case of homesickness. It's perfectly understandable, and forgivable. We were only engaged a day or two, and after working so hard for all those weeks, it only makes sense that you'd look to another man for companionship."

"James," she said, taking both of his hands in her own, "that's not the case. I wish it was that simple, but it isn't."

"Nonsense." James hadn't been touted as

a brilliant attorney without reason. With infuriating ease, he twisted everything she said around to suit his own purposes.

"I love Cody." She said it forcefully enough, she prayed, for James to accept it as truth.

"As I already said, that isn't possible." He stood, placing his hands on her shoulders, his look indulgent. "You love me, remember? Otherwise you wouldn't have agreed to become my wife."

"I agreed to your proposal because I *like* you. And because it pleased my mother and father," she cried.

"Christy." He said her name softly, as if she were a petulant child. "I'm sure you're mistaken."

"I'm not." Her hands on his forearms, she stared directly into his eyes. "I love Cody Franklin so much I married him."

It hurt Christy to watch the transformation come over his face. She hated the pain she saw. The disbelief. The humiliation.

"It's true," she said before he could question her.

Anger flickered in his eyes. He jerked his arms free from her and dropped them to his sides.

"When?"

"Does it matter?"

"No, I guess not." His eyes drifted briefly shut. That said more than any words he could have spoken.

She took a moment to open the clasp of her purse and take out the diamond ring he'd given her. When she handed it back to him, James stared at the velvet box as if he'd never seen it before. "Keep it."

"No, I can't."

He removed it from her hand and turned away long enough to shove it into his coat pocket. When he looked at her again, he was able to mask the pain, but she knew him well enough to realize how deeply she'd hurt him. Causing him such intense suffering was the most difficult thing she'd ever had to do. James didn't deserve to be treated this way.

"I intended to tell you the minute I got home from Montana," she said in her own defense, the words coming so fast they nearly blended together.

"The engagement party," he supplied for her. "You tried to tell me then, didn't you?" He didn't wait for her to answer. "I sensed something was wrong and trapped you into setting a wedding date." He scowled. "On a subconscious level I ignored the obvious, immersed myself in my work, hoping whatever had happened with you would pass. I know I made it difficult to talk to me. But am I that unreasonable that you couldn't have told me the truth?"

"That wasn't it." Christy felt it was important to correct that impression. "I just didn't feel I could. You were so heavily involved in the Mulligan case and I didn't want to —"

"I'm still involved."

"I know. But the worst of it's over, and I couldn't go on pretending. I'm sorry, James, sorrier than you'll ever realize."

He snickered, but didn't openly contradict her.

"I'm terribly fond of you and I'd give anything to —"

"Fond." He spit out the word as if it were an obscenity.

His vehemence was a shock. James wasn't a passionate man. Rarely had Christy seen him reveal any emotion, in or out of a courtroom.

Once more she tried to explain. "I don't expect you to understand how difficult this was for me. That would be asking too much of you." She knew she sounded shaken, but she couldn't help that. "If there was any possible way I could've done this without hurting you, I would have."

He didn't respond.

"You're a wonderful man, James, and

someday a woman will come into your life — the right woman. And you'll know what I mean."

"You were the right woman. Or so I believed."

"I'm sorry. So very sorry."

He shook his head as if he didn't quite believe her. His hand was buried in his pocket, and Christy guessed he'd made a tight fist around the diamond.

"I only wish you the best," she whispered.

He breathed deeply, then nodded, although Christy had the impression he didn't agree with her. She was about to say something more when a thunderous shout came from the direction of the living room.

"Your father?" James asked.

Christy nodded. "Cody must have told him."

James's gaze continued to hold hers. "You'll be all right?"

"Of course."

He seemed to accept that. "Can I kiss you, one last time?"

In response she opened her arms to him, her eyes brimming with unshed tears. James reached for her, his touch gentle. He held her close for just a moment, then pressed his mouth to hers.

He broke away, and his finger touched her

cheek, his eyes clouded. "Be happy, Christy."

"I will."

With that he turned and walked out of the kitchen. Christy stood by the window and watched him move down the walkway, then climb inside his car. For what seemed an eternity, James sat in the driver's seat with his hands gripping the steering wheel as he stared straight ahead.

Christy couldn't delay the confrontation with her family any longer. Squaring her shoulders, she walked into the living room to find her brothers, Paul, Jason and Rich, perched on bar stools as though viewing a stage performance.

"Christy," her mother sobbed, dabbing a tissue under her nose, "tell us it isn't true."

She moved next to Cody and sat on the arm of the chintz-covered chair. She slipped her hand into his. "Cody and I were married last week."

"Married!" Her father stormed to his feet as if she'd desecrated the Constitution of the United States.

Confused, Christy's eyes went to Cody's.

"I hadn't gotten around to telling them that part yet," he told her.

"Married," her mother repeated. "It can't be true. Christy would never do anything so . . . We have a wedding to plan. You couldn't possibly have gone off and gotten married without telling your own mother and father. It isn't like you to do something so underhanded."

"I thought they knew," she whispered, bewildered. "I heard Dad shout, and I thought . . . I assumed."

"All I said," Cody explained, "was that you wanted a little privacy with James so you could return his engagement ring."

"Oh." She swallowed and closed her eyes for a moment. "Well, Mom and Dad," she said brightly, looking at them once more, "I see you've met your new son-in-law."

"Welcome to the family," Paul said, holding up a soft drink can in tribute. "From what Rich said, you're a friend of Russ's."

Cody nodded.

"But you couldn't possibly be married," her mother whimpered, turning to Eric as though he could explain everything.

"Trust me, Mom, we're married."

"They're married," Rich said, saluting them with his own can of soda. "I should know. I was at their wedding night."

"Hear, hear," Jason cried, wearing the ever-present baseball cap. "Wait a minute. At their *wedding* night?"

"I don't find any of this humorous or in

good taste," Eric roared. "Your sister's turned down the best man in three states for some . . . some small-town lawman. Bad enough that Taylor had to marry a country boy, but Christy, too? Never!"

"Dad," Christy reminded him softly, "the deed is done."

"But, Christy," Elizabeth wailed, "I bought the material for the bridesmaids' dresses and we've put down a deposit on the hall for the reception, and —"

"I didn't mean to cheat you out of a wedding, Mom. I really didn't."

"What will we say to our friends?" Her mother appeared to be in a state of shock. She'd gone deathly pale, and her shoulders jerked as she tried to gain control of her emotions.

"If you're worried about what to tell your friends," Paul said, sounding knowledgeable, "I'd suggest the truth."

"Stay out of this," Eric shouted, dismissing his eldest son with a shake of his head. "We're in one hell of a mess here."

"How's that?" Cody asked.

"Christy's married to you is how," Eric informed him none too gently. "My daughter doesn't belong in the country. She was born and raised in the city. We've already got Taylor living out in the sticks. I won't allow Christy to be out there slopping hogs or whatever you do in that backwoods community."

"Dad!" Christy was outraged. "It's *my* decision. And Cougar Point isn't any backwoods community. Besides, we won't be living there."

"You're moving to Washington state?" Elizabeth asked Cody, her eyes wide and hopeful.

"Sorry, no."

Her mother drooped against the back of the sofa and reached for a fresh tissue. She wadded it up and pressed it over her eyes as if to block out this horrible scene.

"Cody's the sheriff," Christy said, wanting to impress both of her parents with the fact that he was a responsible citizen. "We'll be living in Miles City once he's installed."

"A sheriff should please them," Jason said under his breath, speaking to his two brothers.

"I think they prefer an attorney over a sheriff," Rich concluded when neither parent responded to Christy's announcement.

"I recognize that this is all rather abrupt," Cody said in a reasonable voice. "I don't blame you for being shocked. I can't even blame you for being concerned. You wouldn't have raised a daughter as wonderful as Christy if you weren't the kind of people who'd care about her happiness."

"That's good," Paul whispered to Jason. "He's going to win them over with flattery."

"Will you three shut up," Eric yelled, infuriated with his sons and not bothering to disguise it.

"Dad, please try to understand," Christy tried again. "I fell in love with Cody."

"Falling in love is one thing, but marrying him on the sly is another."

"While she was engaged to James, I might add." Rich apparently didn't know when to keep his mouth closed. Both Eric and Cody sent daggers his way. Guarding his face with his hands, Rich pretended to ward off their attack.

"I can only say I love you both," Christy said. "I'd never intentionally do anything to hurt you. In fact, most of my life I've done everything I can to please you, right down to becoming engaged to James."

"I can't believe I'm hearing this," Eric said to his wife. "We raised her the best we knew how, and now this."

"Darling, we thought you loved James," her mother pleaded.

"I thought I did, too, until I met Cody." Her hand clasped Cody's, and she smiled down at him. "I know I made mistakes, lots of them."

"*We* made mistakes," Cody corrected, his gaze holding hers.

"No one's making a list," her father mumbled, "but if I were —"

"Nothing on this earth will ever convince me I made a mistake marrying Cody." Her father obviously wasn't willing to accept what they'd done. As Christy suspected, her family would need time to come to terms with her marriage and the fact that she'd be leaving the Seattle area.

"I gave my week's notice when I returned from vacation," Christy said. It had been one of the low points of her life, telling Marcia she was quitting her job in order to prepare for her wedding. The lie had all but choked her.

"You're leaving your job?"

"She couldn't very well continue working with James," Eric muttered to his wife. "And from the sounds of it, she intends to live in Montana."

"Poor James," Elizabeth said with a regretful sigh. "He would've made such a good husband."

"I'll make Christy a good husband, too," Cody promised. "I love your daughter."

An awkward silence followed Cody's words. "My daughter doesn't belong in

Montana, and she deserves a decent wedding with her family around her. Christy's not the type of girl a man takes to a justice of the peace."

"We were married by a minister." Christy knew even before she spoke that there was little she could say to appease her father. He wasn't accustomed to having his authority challenged. Not even by a sheriff.

"It might be best if we gave your parents a chance to get used to the idea," Cody suggested.

Christy agreed, but leaving her family home was one of the most difficult tasks of her life.

Paul, Jason and Rich followed them outside.

"They'll come around," Paul said to Cody as they exchanged handshakes. Paul was tall and silver-blond, the only one in the family who'd inherited that coloring.

"Just give 'em a year or three," Rich said with less than diplomatic cheer. "Grandkids will be sure to win 'em over. There *will* be children, won't there?" He was eyeing Christy as if a good stare would tell him if she was in the family way.

"Don't worry about a thing," Jason said, throwing his arm over Cody's broad shoulders. "Mom and Dad will accept your marriage before you know it."

"They've got two days," Cody said darkly.

"Two days?" Christy echoed, a little stunned, although she shouldn't have been. Cody's life was in Miles City, and he'd recently taken three days of his vacation to spend with her. He couldn't afford to take off any more, not during this important period of transition.

"Is that too soon for you?" he asked, his eyes revealing his concern. "I figured that would give us enough time to get your things packed and shipped."

She nodded, slipping her arms around his waist. Her life was linked to Cody's now, and there was no turning back.

They hadn't gone through airport security yet, but Christy delayed, glancing around the terminal building, certain if she stayed there long enough her parents would rush in and throw their arms around her, telling her how much they loved her and how they wished her and Cody well.

Only they hadn't come.

"Honey," Cody said patiently. "They aren't coming. We have to go."

"I know, but I'd hoped. I . . . thought they'd at least want to say goodbye."

Christy hadn't heard from them in the two

hectic days they'd spent packing up her apartment. She'd tried not to let it affect her, but she'd always been close to her parents, and being shunned this way hurt more than anything they could have said.

"Give them time," Cody said — he'd been saying that a lot — and it seemed as if her pain belonged to him, too.

Christy offered him a brave smile and nodded.

They joined the security line, then hurried to their departure area, arriving just as their flight was called. Christy realized there was nothing left to do but board the plane that would take her away from everything that was familiar and bring her to a whole new life.

"You're not sorry, are you?" Cody asked once they were seated and about to take off.

"No." Beyond a doubt Christy knew she was meant to be with Cody. She would've preferred to have her parents' blessing. But if she had to do without it, then she'd learn to accept that.

Cody was her love. And now he was her life.

Since Paul, Jason and Rich all worked days and hadn't been able to come to the airport to say their goodbyes, the three of them had taken Christy and Cody to dinner the night before.

Everyone had made an effort to have a good time, and they all had.

Only something vital had been missing. No one said anything. No one had to.

Eric and Elizabeth Manning weren't there. And what was missing was their love. Their blessing. Their approval.

Christy didn't know when she'd see her parents again.

"Oh, Cody," Christy whispered, stepping back to study her husband in his full dress uniform. "You look . . . wonderful."

They'd been in Miles City, Montana, a week. In that time they'd moved into their first home, unpacked their belongings and gone about making a place for themselves in the community.

"When will Russ and Taylor get here?"

"Oh," she said, still a little awed by how handsome Cody looked. "I forgot to tell you Taylor phoned. They're going to meet us at the courthouse for the installation."

"Good." He straightened the sleeves of his crisp uniform jacket. "Well, I'm ready."

"I'm not," Christy told him. "In case you haven't noticed, I'm not dressed yet."

Cody wiggled his eyebrows suggestively.

"All the better to seduce you, my dear."

Christy giggled. "I do believe you've seduced me in every room of this house, Sheriff Franklin. More than once."

"There's time —"

"There most certainly is not." She scurried past him. She wasn't quick enough, and with little effort, Cody caught her in his arms.

"Cody," she warned him. "We . . . can't. You don't want to be late for your own installation. And I don't want to arrive at the ceremony looking like a disheveled mess."

Cody hesitated. "Well . . ."

She entwined her arms around his neck and kissed him soundly.

"Shameless hussy," he said with a grin as he unwound her arms. "Get dressed before I change my mind."

"Yes, sir." Mockingly she saluted him.

A half hour later they entered the courthouse. Judge Carter would be doing the honors, and the room was filled to capacity. Christy was escorted to the front row of reserved seats. Many of the citizens of Cougar Point were in the audience.

The ceremony was about to begin when Taylor, carrying Eric, and Russ slipped into the chairs to her right. That left two empty seats on her left. Christy was so busy greeting her sister that she didn't notice the vacant chairs had been filled. She turned to smile and introduce herself to her seatmates, and to her astonishment saw her parents.

"Mom. Dad." Without warning, tears flooded her eyes. She looked at Cody, who was standing at the podium with Judge Carter. When she nodded toward her family, Cody's face brightened.

"Are you willing to forgive your father for being a stubborn old cuss?" Eric asked in a low voice.

Christy nodded, shaken by the intensity of her relief. She hugged him and then her mother, who was as teary-eyed as Christy.

When the ceremony was over, Cody joined them. Christy's husband and father faced each other. Eric Manning offered his hand first, and the two exchanged a hearty shake.

Judge Carter came forward to introduce himself a few minutes after that, and soon they were all talking at once.

A small reception followed, and Cody held Christy's hand as he led the way.

"Thank you," she whispered.

He shook his head. "Honey, as much as I'd like to take credit for bringing your parents out here, I can't."

294

"Not that," she said, smiling up at him from the very depths of her soul. "Thank you for loving me."

"That," he said softly, "was the easiest thing I've ever done."

"Eric Manning," Christy could hear her father say over the din of raised voices. "I'm the sheriff's father-in-law. We're proud of the boy. Glad to have him in the family."

"Not as glad as he is to be part of it," Cody murmured, smiling at his wife.

ABOUT THE AUTHOR

Debbie Macomber, the author of *Back on Blossom Street, A Good Yarn, Susannah's Garden* and *6 Rainier Drive,* has become a leading voice in women's fiction worldwide. Her work has appeared on every major bestseller list, including those of the *New York Times, USA TODAY* and *Publishers Weekly.* She is a multiple award winner, and won the 2005 Quill Award for Best Romance. More than sixty million copies of her books have been sold worldwide. For more information on Debbie and her books, visit her Web site at www.DebbieMacomber.com.

We hope you have enjoyed this Large Print book. Other Thorndike, Wheeler, and Chivers Press Large Print books are available at your library or directly from the publishers.

For information about current and upcoming titles, please call or write, without obligation, to:

Publisher
Thorndike Press
295 Kennedy Memorial Drive
Waterville, ME 04901
Tel. (800) 223-1244

or visit our Web site at:

http://gale.cengage.com/thorndike

OR

Chivers Large Print
published by BBC Audiobooks Ltd
St James House, The Square
Lower Bristol Road
Bath BA2 3SB
England
Tel. +44(0) 800 136919
email: bbcaudiobooks@bbc.co.uk
www.bbcaudiobooks.co.uk

All our Large Print titles are designed for easy reading, and all our books are made to last.